A MEDIEVAL THRILLER

THE GOOD KING

GEORGE WB SCOTT

Black Rose Writing | Texas

The author grants the final approval for this literary material.

First printing

This is a work of fiction. Names, characters, businesses, places, events, and incidents are either the products of the author's imagination or used in a fictitious manner. Any resemblance to actual persons, living or dead, or actual events is purely coincidental.

ISBN: 978-1-68513-358-0
PUBLISHED BY BLACK ROSE WRITING
www.blackrosewriting.com

Printed in the United States of America
Suggested Retail Price (SRP) $18.95

The Good King is printed in Minion Pro

*As a planet-friendly publisher, Black Rose Writing does its best to eliminate unnecessary waste to reduce paper usage and energy costs, while never compromising the reading experience. As a result, the final word count vs. page count may not meet common expectations.

PRAISE FOR
The Good King, A Medieval Thriller

"Two brothers chose different paths. One led to sainthood; the other to hell...Intrigue, murder, and a lifelong quest for redemption. This is the stuff of legends!"
–Karen Brees, author of
Crosswind: The WWII Adventures of MI6 Agent Katrin Nissen

"An absolute tour de force. I was enraptured by a story of politics, religion, family, and betrayal. Anyone who enjoys historical fiction will absolutely fall in love with this book, just as I have."
–*The Faerie Review*

"A gruesome tale of crime and redemption set in 10th century Bohemia... vivid and compelling."
–Anna Engelsone, author of *Fool For An Heir*

"This is a well-written story... The American reader will find a thorough and entertaining lesson on the origins of Christianity in medieval Bohemia and, finally, an understanding of the famous Christmas song 'Good King Wenceslas.'"
–Dr. Petr Kubín, Department of Ecclesiastical History and
Literary History, Charles University, Prague, Czech Republic

"St. Wenceslas is the patron saint of my country and I feel a deep reverence for him. I would like to say a big thank you. You inspired me..."
–Hana Konvalinková, Political, Environmental, Social Activist,
Filmmaker, English Instructor, Zlín, Czech Republic

"Who was King Wenceslas? *The Good King* goes a long way to answering this question. A fantastic job of describing life in the 10th century with lots of period details."
–Jean M. Roberts, author of *The Heron* and *The Angel of Goliad*

"You had me hooked... the brother of 'Good King Wenceslas!' Contrasting Ludmila and Dragomira... they are both such strong, powerful, influential females."
–Vandy Kemp, Educational Consultant
and Former Dean of Students, Maryville College

To all the saints we know
who make our world a better place.

AUTHOR'S NOTE TO THE READER

That carol "Good King Wenceslas" has haunted my interest since I first heard it as a boy growing up in South Florida. The concept of snow "deep and crisp and even" was enthralling and unimaginable. That idyllic scene is one happy element in the saint's tragic chronicle.

The book in your hand is not a happy Christmas story.

This dark tale happens at the very beginning of written history—and literacy—in the Czech-speaking duchy of medieval Bohemia. There are very few documents from the period, and those existing are usually contradictory. Sparse church records were often written a generation or more after the events described. They embellish the basic story with miracles attributed to saints and usually are cluttered with language complimenting the ancestors of the document's audience.

Because of this, as an author of fiction I can create a new story line and still be within the historical record, such as it is.

Academic papers gave me the background of lives of common people and nobility, customs, worship, food crops, etc. Some elements of Czech folk traditions are also included.

Life was brutal in the early middle ages. There was little regard for what today we call human rights, and no apparent concept of love and romance. I do not attempt to soothe modern sensibilities, and I try not to over-sensationalize the most brutal elements in the story—reality was plenty brutal enough.

This is primarily written for an English-speaking audience, and not speaking Czech myself, I use very little of that language. I employ some Czech names and concepts to achieve credulity within the range of fiction. Many characters and events are historical, though the original sources often provide little beyond their names. For fictional characters, I've made my best attempt at appropriate Czech terms and names.

For "Dragomira," the mother of Boleslav I and Saint Wenceslas, the Czech spelling may be closer to "Drahomira." I use a more emotionally evocative (to an English-speaking readership) Polish spelling. Other non-Czech names may apply to characters who came from outside Bohemia.

Anachronistic dangers abound. I use universal alternatives to modern measurements such as the length of a finger, so many paces, etc.

Chapters use Czech names of months, together with a meaning of the name. They are not in annual order, but apply times of year to elements of chapters they designate.

This is an all too human tale of anguish, murder and saintly grace, of betrayal, loyalty and revenge. It presents an exploration of a universal search for spiritual fulfillment.

I also hope to encourage thought and interest in a foundational nation important to Western thought and culture.

-George WB Scott

THE
GOOD
KING

Sins of my youth remember not,
   Neither my trespasses;
After thy mercy mind thou me
   O Lord, my god, for thy goodness.

From Psalm 25

CHAPTER 1
Leden—The Time of Ice

He Named Me Dreadful

I write this record six years after the meeting I herein describe. I am older now, and can see more clearly. Long years of study are ahead of me, yet I must take time to document these days of my youth when my father told me the reason for my life's mission, and to reflect on faith, love, justice, and duty.

***

In the cold winter of the year of our Lord 947, I was called to meet with my father before my journey from our capital of Prague to the Church center of Regensburg. I had been raised in a different town, where I was tutored by a Christian priest to dedicate my life to Godly work. And I was to continue learning the ways of the Faith, my letters, and how better to pray—especially for Father.

His summons filled me with apprehension. I had heard dark whispers of his youth.

My father is Boleslav, Duke of all Bohemia, ancient land of the Czech people. He strove to live a Godly life, and still continues to, but in his anguish and despair he was given to excesses and, in his soul's agony, drank more from his winecup than he should.

He was tortured in his heart and soul despite years of good works to establish churches and monasteries all over Bohemia. He feared when he died he would never see Heaven. He told me he needed my prayers to help him enter that blessed land when his time on earth was done.

I lived at the castle of Tetín with my mother, where my grandmother Ludmila had lived, and where she died. My visit to Castle Prague would be our final meeting before my journey to continue my education, and eventual consecration in the Church. I expected the duke's kind blessing, but he gave me something else.

***

Winter had come on our land, and the dark, early days of the year were upon us. I set out at first light with two servants and a horse loaded with my books, my traveling goods, letters and funds.

The ground was frozen, and all was still on the evening we arrived at Hrad Prague. Lights in the castle shone from the windows on the evening we arrived and were visible from the city. Our horses carefully climbed the icy street, and we walked through the gates into the home of my father.

The house servants welcomed us from the cold into the somewhat warmer castle. I was fed in the warm kitchen, and I was shown my room. My serving man and the groom were sent to eat with the palace servants and would sleep in the stable. We would stay at the hrad for three nights before beginning our journey to the lands of the Franks. I was eager to see the city of Regensburg, but I knew the journey would be cold and unpleasant.

My older brother, named after our father, greeted me when I entered, and we shared a brief conversation. He was entering his prime years now and had a fine beard. My brother would become duke in his time, when Father died. He would become Boleslav II. His words to me were courteous, yet he seemed more stern than I remembered him, and his eyes peered into mine in curious inquiry. He put his hand on my head, gently and firmly, as if to show he was stronger and taller. And he wore a large knife on his belt.

Father's page Tira came for me. He was a serious man, about Father's age or a little older.

Young Boleslav turned to leave, and after two steps paused and gave a brief backward glance at me.

***

Tira led me to the main hall where Father was conferring with counselors and clerics. Candles and an oil lamp lit the room. The men sat by the fire discussing the land's business. Father's fur robes were folded back over his chair, not needed in the room's warmth. His small dog was curled in his lap.

Father saw me and waved me over. He looked tired and worn. He was in his thirty-eighth year, the twelfth of his rule, and his face was still firm, if lined with care. His beard was streaked with gray, and he still had most of his teeth. I expected that I would look much like him twenty-six years later.

He told his counselors to leave. My audience was to be private. Old Tira gave me a wan smile as he left. I did not feel at ease in the duke's presence.

This evening he had not yet drunk much, and his mood was somber. He directed me to a place by the fire and had me sit. After a draw from his flagon, he spoke to me.

"Hello, Dreadful Feast," he said.

He had not called me that name in years. I felt the hair rise on my neck.

I am called Kristián now.

"I want to speak with you before you begin your journey. We are denied any future we can see, and for all we know, we may not meet again in this world."

This was an ominous greeting.

I sat before him. His small dog leapt from his lap and sniffed my hand.

"I gave you the name 'Dreadful Feast' twelve years ago because of an old custom: 'Give a child a false name so a demon won't find him.' I hope no demon finds you. Demons certainly found me." He paused and sipped from his cup.

"Sometimes I am sorry I named you that, but in another way I am glad I did. It minds me of my sins. We all call you 'Kristián' now, because you must be more Christian than all of us. Especially more than I. But never forget your original name!

"It is time I told you why I named you that."

He set his flagon on the table near his hand, and when a slave had fed the fire behind him, he turned his head and gazed into the embers. His right hand rested on his breast, over his heart.

He recited a few lines from a psalm he had memorized as a child:

"Sins of my youth remember not,
Neither my trespasses."

He glanced again into the glowing coals.

"I want you to know your ancestry, and how we came to be leaders of the Czechs, of our land of Bohemia. In some future time, our blood may grow great beyond this land.

"I will be frank with you, because you must grasp the complete tale of how I came to my distress. If you know all, you can better intercede for me, with God.

"I will be honest.

"You will not like much of what you hear."

So began his tale, and in it he bared his life to me. He spoke as if I were a priestly confessor instead of his twelve-year-old son. I did not interrupt my father's story, even when his words were disturbing.

Though I was in awe of him, the life task he placed on me was to save his soul from Hell. He began to tell me why.

Kristián my son, I became duke when my older brother Václav died, who some now call by a Latinized name, "Wenceslas." The tale of his death is bound up with your name. My mother's tale is bound up in me, and my grandmother's too. We are all the sums of our fathers and mothers, and their fathers and mothers, and of the very earth itself.

We do not choose our ancestors, our families, nor the land where we are born. Ours is a wonderful land. Never doubt it.

I have finally learned I can choose my friends. Perhaps I learned too late, or almost too late. History will decide. Choose your friends well!

I know you have spent your childhood learning the ways of the Church. I can't tell you our entire history, but I'll tell you a bit of it. All that has happened before was told to us by our forbearers, from what was spoken to them. What happens now, and after, may be written for all time. Our generations are on the edge of history.

When I look back on my life, I wonder what it was for. Is it the lot of a man to do what he must to overcome others in the world or perhaps to just survive? Some say we are set on earth with a purpose, to help our fellow man. That's what my brother thought, what he taught our people.

His final act was to teach me that as he died. I took up his purpose to bring Christianity to this land.

As duke, or king, or ruler, my days may be ended at any time, by blade or poison, disease, or something unknown. God may just call me home. So, sit here with me, Son, and hold my little dog, Mazel. I named him because he likes to cuddle.

I had a different sort of education than you. Much different.

***

They told me I was born in mid-winter, the year after the great invasion by the Magyars. They didn't invade us here in Prague because my father's king was already paying tribute to their king, as we were invaded before and had to make peace. But the Frankish kingdom hadn't been invaded in a long time, and they were surprised. The forces of their Christian god were no match for those horse-riding pagans.

We had our own gods then, different from those the Magyars worshipped, but more like them than the god the German-speaking Franks were forcing on us. The same Christian god Who I build churches for now.

The Franks to our north and west had long pressed us here in Bohemia and sent armies against us and the rest of the Kingdom of

Great Moravia. We could hold them off sometimes and even raid their lands. But those Magyars with their far-shooting bows didn't fight like Franks. Unlike them, the Magyars were lightly armed and moved quickly. They ruined the strength of the Franks at the Battle of Lechfeld by fooling the Franks into chasing them into ambush, where the might of the Franks was destroyed. Then the Magyars rampaged for weeks, far into Frankish lands before returning to their home country.

There was lots of raiding in those years, by Franks, Magyars, Varangians, and by other Slavic tribes like our own Czech people. Things are peaceful now, though we must pay tribute to the Franks. Our part of the Moravian kingdom was at peace then, though impoverished by payments to the Magyars. And so, that's the world I was born into.

I was named Boleslav, which means "Greater Glory." My older brother was named Václav, born three years earlier, whose name also means "Greater Glory." I used to wonder which of us was to be greater.

Oh, I know.

I want to share with you the foundation of our story. You may know some of it from your Frankish tutor, but you should get a Czech view of it.

Our lands first became Christian when my grandfather, twenty-two years old and in the prime of his manhood, journeyed with his escort to visit the Moravian king. The new king of Great Moravia held a banquet and invited all his vassal dukes, including Grandfather, a royal descendant of our humble ancestor Přemysl the Plowman.

The Christian faith had come to our land centuries before with Irish and English missionaries, but people mostly ignored it and kept to their older religion, the one I was raised in. We worshipped mighty Svantovít and the other gods. The kings of the Franks along with their church bishops sought to gain greater power over us and sent their Christian missionaries to convert us.

The Frankish priests spoke their German language among themselves. They told our people we must obey their new Christian rules because it was the Word of God, and they condemned those who disobeyed to Hell. They could describe Hell in German and in our language. That was no problem for them.

We Czechs have always been reluctant to give others power over us, and our Moravian king petitioned the Church of Rome for a bishop who was not under Frankish control. He was refused. Then he sent to the Eastern Church in Constantinople to ask the Greek Christian Church for help. There had been increasing friction between Constantinople and Rome for decades, and the Church of Christ was in the throes of an irreversible split.

The prelate of that church, in the old empire of the Caesars, was head of the Christian church in Constantinople. He set in play a miracle still living today, which may continue for a thousand generations.

The Byzantine Empire's lands included those with a language similar to ours and other Slavic peoples. Two brothers, proven missionaries, had grown up in a city at the northern edge of their empire, bordering on Slavonic speaking lands. They were Greek speakers themselves, but many in their town spoke a Slavic tongue, and the brothers leaned both languages.

The brothers were sent to Great Moravia, and they took with them the Gospels, written in Greek.

There was no written alphabet for any Slavic language. The brother we know as Cyril developed writing for the Slavic peoples by adapting the Greek phonetic alphabet to our language, adding new letters where Greek ones did not approximate sounds we use. The brothers translated the Gospels and the Psalms into writing in our tongue, the first such written language for uncounted thousands of Slavic peoples. Their alphabet for our language or ones based on it is now used in many nations.

Inventing a way for people to read the Bible for themselves did not please the Frankish priests. People who could read would understand the holy words from more than eight hundred years ago and learn their meaning, without foreign priests translating for them just bits they wanted them to hear—the very words of Christ Himself.

This creation of Cyril helped us and other nations begin a written literature and to share ideas, to become more modern. Before this, our non-Christian priests used only runes and symbols for their magic and worship. Now, those who learned to read could study the Bible, and could write their thoughts in our own language.

Well, my grandfather the duke, your great-grandfather, arrived at the Moravian king's capital and was invited to dine. In the hall, the king and his court were seated at a table, but the Bohemians were directed to sit on the floor.

The king told the duke that custom—apparently a new custom—was for Christians to eat at the table and non-Christians—pagans, as they called our people—must eat on the floor. The duke protested this, and the brother of Cyril, the blessed Saint Methodius himself who was attending, felt pity for him, or perhaps opportunity. He came to speak to the duke and explained the difference between Christians and pagans—more than just where we eat!

The duke asked why he could not become Christian. Methodius told him nothing stood in his way, and he must accept the message of Christ with his whole heart. The next day Grandfather and his thirty-man escort undertook the ritual of fasting, heard the Gospels, and he and his men were baptized into the new faith.

Grandfather brought that Christian faith back to Prague. His wife, my grandmother Ludmila, was baptized some months later by Svatý Methodius.

Grandfather and Grandmother saw the power of the new religion and the benefits it would bring our people. It meant giving some power to whatever Eastern bishop would be over our church, which would not be the Frankish bishop. But it also meant closer relations to a great nation, one with wider trade, with inventions and advantages we did not have here.

Grandfather and Grandmother Ludmila became enthusiastic missionaries of Christianity to the people of Czech. In a passion they rushed to bring people of our lands into the new faith. They started the work of converting people, and they destroyed statues and shrines of the old gods. Many were not pleased. A big change is a shock to people, and they weren't ready to throw out all their beliefs for a new and foreign religion.

The people of Bohemia revolted and drove the duke and Grandmother away to the court of the Moravian king. The people chose another to reign, a cousin of Grandfather's, but he ruled by whim and was too harsh. They put him out and brought back Grandfather and Grandmother Ludmila with the understanding they should be more gentle regarding the people's old religion. My grandparents then ruled more wisely; they slowly brought forth Christian beliefs. But there was no stopping the changes for the people of Bohemia. A religion of written scripture has great power.

When the Frankish king saw the influence of Constantinople's missionaries among the people of Moravia, he deposed and killed the Moravian king. He put a relative of the dead king on the throne, who promised to more closely follow Frankish commands.

Killing and replacing a country's leader is sort of a tradition in this part of the world. Oh, probably everywhere else, too. That act eventually shattered what power Moravia had and forced Bohemia to stand up as an independent duchy. We now rely on our own strength and alliances to defend ourselves.

Here in Prague, the Franks drove out priests of the Greek church and made the Roman church dominant among the converted. The most able of the ousted clerics emigrated to the land of Bulgars, where they were welcomed. They spread their version of Eastern Christianity and their alphabet to other Slavic tribes, to the Rus and beyond. From that time forward in Bohemia the Czechs worshipped in the rites of the Roman church, though many read the Slavonic Gospel translations of Cyril.

Kristián, I am telling you this background so you will see the tensions that gripped this land. The land I am shaping into a modern nation must withstand the challenges all rulers must face. Your brother must hold this land someday.

My grandfather continued his work preparing for defense of our lands. He helped Ludmila found churches and schools to spread the Word, still using the Slavonic translations of Methodius and Cyril, which the Church in Rome recognizes as one of its ecumenical languages.

My grandparents' marriage was a good one. When Grandfather became a Christian, Grandmother Ludmila took to the new religion with a passion. She saw the appeal of the religion, its order, and its message of peace and love. And it has a nice story behind it, at least in the Gospels.

This is the greatest reason the religion was successful. Its principal message of love and forgiveness is what most people want.

Ludmila was a pious student of the Bible and the message of Christ Jesus. She was active in other fields as well.

Our Czech land is mostly forested, with scattered towns and small clearings where people tend their barley, millet, beets, wheat, poppies, flax. I'm sure you have seen some of that. Our land makes lots of honey, too. Ludmila learned of new crops and shared them with the people. She encouraged the tending of fruit trees and all manner of beneficial crops. It was as if Ludmila embodied the person of Kazi, one of the three daughters of Krok of generations before, with her ancient knowledge of plants, trees, and herbs.

Some people in the towns converted to Christianity, some pretended to because it pleased my grandparents. But the people weren't pleased with new rules that came with the faith. Many still kept more than one wife, and worshipped their traditional gods deep in the woods. They would feign Christianity in the towns, but still gather beneath holy Linden trees and Oaks in sacred groves to burn sacrifices and sing hymns to the old gods. In hallowed clearings in the wild forests they would dance the kolo and freely share their bodies with each other. They made sacrifices and fires, and prayed and practiced magic. They sang hymns to gods and goddesses who lived in the sky and forests and rivers and mountains.

The pagan priests were important, and not just for soothing people afflicted by a god's displeasure or someone's curse. For important services, the priest sacrificed wild boars at holy springs, or at the junction of rivers to let the blood mix with the water to bless it. At harvest they put food about the foot of the image of their god Svantovít and filled his horn with mead. The god was sometimes portrayed with multiple heads to show his different powers, and that he is ever watchful.

If the honey wine in his cup lasted for several days, they believed the next year would have good harvests.

The people built bonfires and danced in a circle around it in celebrations for the goddess of fertility. They lusted in dales and hollows and practiced ancestral magic, and they reveled and sang.

Another pagan custom is at the death of a man, his body is burned on a great pyre. The fire's ashes and smoke mix with his as it rises to the moon and stars—where all properly burnt souls go to live forever in the sky. As Christians, people learned to bury their dead, though some still wanted to crush their skulls. Dead bodies that weren't burned could retain their souls and walk again without this precaution, or so the old customs said.

Many in our land held on to habits of our ancestors even as we were being drawn into the demanding influence of Christendom, with its promises of glory, a message of peace, rules for good behavior—and with a firm hand from the Frankish priests.

When the duke finally died, his eldest son took the throne, and when he died without heirs, the ducal throne fell to his younger brother, my father. He was already married to Mother, a princess of a tribe of Slavs to the north. Her name was Dragomira.

Father was given the haircutting ceremony, shown the work boots of our ancestor Přemysl the Farmer, and was invested as duke.

Dragomira means, well, peace and love, or "love of peace." She didn't, though. Our household was not peaceful.

Mother beat the servants, including my wetnurse Saskia. I always saw scars on her shoulders while she was nursing me. Mother had her nurse me past what most mothers do. She made her feed me her body's milk until my ninth year—and then later once more...

Mother held absolute control over Saskia, and used her and others to control me. Eventually, I committed the act that made me name you, my son, my unblemished, blessed and cursed son, "Strachkvas," or "Dreadful Feast," to remind me of my heinous sin.

But I don't call you that now. I call you "Kristián."

Call a servant to refill my cup. I want to tell you more.

My father turned back to the fire as I stood up. The little dog followed me to the door, where a maidservant was waiting. I gave her the duke's order, and she left for the kitchen.

I walked over to a window and looked out on the plaza.

The night was dark and cold beyond the castle walls. In the distance, a few bundled figures moved at the edge of the trees. They were shadows, black against a snowy starlit ground. I wondered if they were traveling toward their homes, or scavenging what they could find along the edge of the forest.

Some of the history that Father told me I had learned from my tutor, but my teacher is a Frank, and told me more about the German lands than my own. The legends of Czech and of Krok's daughters are part of our land's history, and Mother and her maids had told me those. I cared little about the politics of religion at my age then. There was peace, and I enjoyed it without knowing I should worry about it.

My older brother stayed with Father and was being groomed for rule. He learned swordcraft and Czech history. I studied Latin letters.

Before returning, I looked at Father sitting by the fire. His hand was rubbing his chest again, just over his heart. He gazed into the fire's embers and seemed to ponder a memory, or perhaps the eternal punishment he feared.

The maid returned with a jug, and Mazel and I followed her back into my father's company.

Father leaned back in the chair and straightened his shirt. He began more of his tale.

Kristián, my grandmother Ludmila saw the draw of Christ's words, a message that could lead the entire world of humanity to peace and love. I think she was innocent and naïve enough to believe it.

My elder brother Václav, heir to the Czech lands, was born at the ancient castle Hrad Stochov near Libušín, where our ancestors ruled in ages past. While he was still very young, Mother took him to visit Grandmother Ludmila at her castle of Hrad Tetín, where Ludmila had planted trees. One oak is said to have been watered with by brother's bathwater. I'm sure you have seen it. It's large, and growing vigorously.

Father was called "duke," but to all purposes he was king. The ruler of Great Moravia, of which Bohemia was a part, was weak.

When Father married Dragomira, she converted to Christianity— or told Father she had. But Mother was not a Christian.

One thing Mother hated about the Christian religion was Jesus wanted people to be peaceful, to show love to everyone. She believed peaceful people could not survive in the world. She also saw it as a way for outside prelates to have control over our people, which it surely is.

The new religion has rules and beliefs our old religion does not have, such as a man should keep only one woman as a wife. The act of physical intercourse is itself sinful under most conditions, and we are born sinful and must ask the Church for forgiveness and salvation. So by adopting the Christian religion, our children are already obligated to the Church at birth! I am not sure I believe that. I have known sinless children who did not know Christ.

Christians say there is only one god, not many, though God has three parts. I still don't quite understand that part of it. They say the world was created over a period of several days, not all at once. They tell the people when a man dies, his soul and all feeling leave the body upon death and don't linger there, or at least not long. These are some differences, and many did not want to change from the ways of our fathers. And accepting Christianity includes the belief in damnation.

The new religion was all written down and confirmed through the Church's hierarchy. The old religion had only symbols, runes interpreted by priests who could bend them to say anything. That happens with Christian priests, too, but if one can read, you can always go back to the words in the Book.

Václav learned to read young. I never really did. I have a clerk tell me what the marks mean in documents I receive or must sign.

The holy books of the Frankish Christian religion are written in Latin, a language unintelligible to common people. They had to rely on Frankish priests to interpret the new rules of Christianity. Czechs speaking Slavonic must hear Germans interpret Latin translations of the original Greek and Hebrew. And of course, they interpreted them to support the Frankish laws.

Your uncle Václav learned his studies and languages, Latin and Greek, and how to read the alphabet given to us by Saint Cyril and Saint Methodius, so he could read the bible in our language. Those are holy words the Teacher spoke Himself, not interpreted by Frankish tools of empire, nor petty priests seeking dominance over sheepish people. They were words spoken by Jesus to his disciples and to the throngs in sermons he gave to common folk, and were meant for everyone. His actual words. Continue your studies, and read them yourself!

When I was an infant, my older brother Václav was already beginning to learn his letters, and was learning his Christian catechism too, in simple rhymes. Father was away at the wars again, and Václav often lived with Grandmother in her home in Tetín. When I was old enough, I sometimes visited. We spent weeks there, just a few hours' ride south and west of Prague. I think Mother was glad to get us out of her house for a while.

Mother had a strong will. She was a daughter of an important chieftain, and she was married to my father to make an alliance between Bohemia and his tribe, even though she was about ten years his senior.

When I married your mother, she was older than I was by more than that.

Raids from many competing tribes and kingdoms meant we had to form arrangements for mutual defense, and often ties of blood are the best way to secure bonds of mutual protection, if not friendship.

As I grew, I learned blood does not guarantee mutual protection, or even survival. Sometimes it just means blood. Oh, Kristián, I've seen too much of it!

When my father—who was a good Christian—and Mother married, she and her servants were baptized, and all wore a cross pendant when she thought they should. But she continued to meet with priests of Svantovít and with holy women in sacred groves near our castle. She often took me with her.

I learned of the god of light and thunder, Svantovít upon his white horse, and Veles, god of waters and cattle, of wealth. My friends and I watched their priests sacrifice wriggling pigs, and cast grain on waters where a stream joined the Vltava. We sang hymns while a priest burned sacred herbs to ensure a good harvest of honey. And we learned the other tales, about ogres and fairies, of tree spirits and about the Eternal Green Hunter Lord walking deep woods with his fang knife in his belt and his wolf-dog ranging about him.

Sometimes deep in the forest we even saw him, or believed we did.

Father ruled well, though not long enough. He built the Christian basilica in Prague and helped draw Bohemia away from the crumbling Great Moravian kingdom, now losing its power and land to outside attacks, and to the Franks. Father sought to bring unity to his realm.

Mother gave him six children, including Václav and myself.

Today many call Václav by the Latinized style of his name, "Wenceslas." I wonder what they will call me after I'm gone.

Despite having children together, I don't think Father much enjoyed being around Mother. She tried to command him—I guess because she was older and very strong willed. He was often away at war, or on diplomacy missions, or just staying at another home away from her.

When Father was home from other towns in our land or from the wars, Václav, hungry for knowledge, asked him for more books and for more instruction than Grandmother Ludmila and her priest could give. Václav seemed to want to learn everything about the world.

The wars seemed constant. Father's name, Vratislav, means "Return with Glory," a name he wanted to live up to. He continued the wars, defending and raiding against our enemies, until finally he was killed in battle. That meant my older brother Václav, raised largely by our Christian grandmother Ludmila, would become duke when he reached his majority. Unless he died.

***

As dowager widow of Grandfather, Grandmother Ludmila was known as "Christ's Handmaiden," because of all her good works. She still lived in the Tetín palace where she and Grandfather retired when my uncle assumed the throne. Her Christian priest ministered to her spiritual journey.

Grandmother spent much effort to bring new farming methods to our people. She brought new ways of making cheese, and spread viticulture to our lands for winemaking, where in the past people had drunk only mead and beer. She brought new varieties of wheat and other plants and flowers and trees.

When Václav was older, he traveled with her and helped plant vineyards. The vines would produce grapes and wine for future generations. They expanded cultivation of barley and hops.

Everyone spoke of how Václav loved learning, and how bright and kind he was, that he was such a beautiful child. I grew weary of hearing how wonderful my older brother was, and that I should be more like him.

He would be duke one day. I was the second son, so I would not.

In those days, Grandmother Ludmila's home wasn't called a "palace." It was a simple wood and thatch house like everyone else's, except it was on the hill above the town, and had a second story and many more rooms, some with whitewashed walls. When I became duke, I built the stone foundation castle we have today here in Prague.

It was a simpler time then. Simpler in many ways.

My beautiful older brother was favored, and was given lots of attention by our Grandmother Ludmila, whose name means "love of the people." And she did love her people, and she loved Václav. And she loved me too, I suppose. But she took Václav to live with her.

She became an influence of Christian goodness on Václav, and he followed her example.

Grandmother taught me those ways as well when I was with her. We would go to her chapel and pray to God, and learn the Gospels and Psalms. Like Václav, I was baptized at birth and Grandmother ensured, when she was present, we both were brought up learning the words of Jesus and teachings of the Psalms and Gospels.

Václav's first words were rhymes taught him by our Grandmother Ludmila, drawn from the Gospels and Psalms translated by our saints Methodius and Cyril.

One he taught me is:

"The Lord to me a Shepherd is, and want shall not I,
He in the folds of tender grass does make me down to lie.
To waters still He gently leads and restores my soul does He;
He does in paths of righteousness, for His name's sake lead me."

Grandmother had lots of those verses converted into rhyme for him to memorize. He taught me some of them. That was early though, before the great change in my childhood.

Of course, as princes we also had our martial studies, and we learned to ride and fight. I looked up to my brother, older and stronger than I was.

Our sisters were brought up differently than Václav and me. They were raised to become wives, to be married to future chiefs and leaders of tribes and countries, those the duke wanted to court for alliances. That is how Mother came to marry Father. Our youngest brother died as an infant, but my sisters were married off to dukes and lords to the east. This helped firm up alliances and trade, and I married your mother, who was a daughter of a noble from a tribe of Mělník.

Generations ago, girls grew up doing most everything men could do. They hunted, rode, plowed, and made decisions for their families. But some men, perhaps fearing weakness in themselves, thought women should act differently. Many women were not happy being ordered about by men.

Once some women took arms and rose up in war to drive away all the men around them, the "War of the Maidens." They built a castle for themselves and lived in it, swearing oaths of loyalty to each other. Men marched to the castle and were driven off, but finally they stormed the castle and killed most of the women. They made the rest slaves and wives. Women have since remained enslaved in some way, and will always remain subservient to men, I suppose. Or they may rise again. Some have a nature that resists servility.

My Grandmother Ludmila was a remarkable woman, strong in her Christian way, a natural leader of people.

Mother Dragomira had a different sort of strength, and taught us other ways.

Unknown to Grandmother, when Václav was living with us, Mother took us to the ancient sacred glade in the forest where we joined services by the local priest, not a Christian. His name was Dušan, which means "Soul." The Church calls these ceremonies "satanic," but no, they were mostly peaceful and fun, with bonfires and circle dancing, songs and feasting, sometimes with sacrifices of chickens or goats, lambs or pigs.

Rites for the gods can make a big impression on a child. Mother knew this.

Václav went to these services with Mother and me, but he didn't participate much. He held to Grandmother's faith.

***

Václav continued to ask for books, and finally, at Mother's urging, Father agreed to send Václav away to school at Budeč. There was a learned priest who would teach him the basics of letters in Latin, so he could better learn and share the ways of the greater world. There were few books in the translations of Cyril at the time. My brother became proficient in Greek as well, and continued his Bible studies in all three languages throughout his whole life.

Before he left, Grandmother Ludmila took him into Prague. Václav was about ten years old, and he told me of this day when I was older.

Grandmother and my brother walked by the Jewish quarter to where captured slaves were being bought and sold. A company of Magyar raiders had captured a village of heathen Poles near our borders. Every hut in their village was burned, and all livestock herded to villages and farms of the raiders. They completely eradicated the hamlet except for the blackened pits in the earth where their homes had been.

They led captives from the village to Prague. When prisoners are brought to our city, if they are not Christian, they are often sold at the slave market.

Václav and Grandmother watched the procession of women and children without passion.

These captives were not the duke's subjects and there was no reason to deny the sales. They had been taken in a foreign land by other men, then brought here. All those sold at the market are pagan, though there are exceptions and lax enforcement, especially regarding peasants bound to the land. When a man's property was appropriated or sold, those slaves went with it. Prague and the duke receive a bounty of gold and silver or other wealth from sales of slaves. So it is profitable, if not really a "good" business.

Kristián, this is my opinion. You will find others who believe holding people in slavery is good as the natural order.

Prague is known throughout the region for its slave market. Many Christians see these practices as brutal. The god Svantovít seems to approve.

Prague was nominally Christian then. Jews, Christians and Muslims, all members of Abrahamic faiths, generally keep no slaves who share those Old Testament traditions. Trading of pagan captives holds no such restrictions, and there has always been a demand for slaves. Christians and non-Christians buy them, and many are bought and sold for the rulers of Spanish Andalusia and Syria, followers of the prophet Mohammed.

Jewish traders have established routes of commerce all over the known world. They trade all manner of goods, including slaves. Prague is a stop on a branch of the Great Road leading from Europe to the ends of the earth, where people and animals are strange.

Several times, I saw very dark-skinned merchants from Spain or Venice. They choose from the captured fair-skinned boys and women those they bring back to Moorish masters.

There is something curious about male slaves wanted for the Spanish Caliphate of Cordoba, or Syria, or Egypt and other Mohammedan places. The emirs, princes, leading citizens and wealthy traders desire boys and young men who are altered so they cannot produce children, and so won't strongly resist enslavement. Some captive boys are so completely castrated that they have no male organ left at all, and most of these do not survive the operation. But those who live fetch a premium price, higher than beautiful women.

In some households, if a slave takes up the religion of his master, he may be granted more rights than unbelieving slaves. Girls and women are sold for concubines and household servants. Many are eventually freed and continue to serve in faraway lands, and some marry and make a life. Some enslaved women bear children for their masters and are considered wives, and when the master dies, they have their freedom.

Of course, many of the male slaves cannot make children.

I sometimes wonder where we will find slaves, after all Slavs become Christian. There are still pagan folks in the far north of Finland, and lands of the Rus. Or perhaps they will be captured in strange lands far to the east, in India, or perhaps Africa far to the south.

Several boys between twelve and sixteen years old were sold as laboring slaves. Some captives were younger boys, pulled from the rest to be taken to the house of surgery where they would become eunuchs, and likely die.

Two boys who were only four years old looked exhausted, but still shocked by seeing their baby siblings, fathers and grandparents killed and their houses looted and burned, and their mothers and sisters roughly violated and taken away. They had no concept of what lay before them, and their tears were of helpless and childish ignorance.

The others were between seven and ten years old. These knew their world had ended. Most silently submitted and were led to the house of surgery, and likely death.

One seven-year-old, tall for his age, had a clear eye and a stronger heart, and looked about him to seek an escape. His captors had bound his hands and hobbled his ankles. There was no avoiding his doom.

Ludmila and Václav came to the line of prisoners and looked into the faces of the captives. Many women had seen their infant children killed. They had already been ravished and were resigned to whatever sad fate awaited them.

Lives of women have always been hard.

The girls of all ages would learn of life in faraway lands. They would learn a new language and skills, and live in Tunisia, or Syria, or with Spanish Moors. Many would produce children and leave a line of Slavic descent in the lands of Arabs. I hear of blue-eyed Egyptians descended from such unions.

The seven-year-old captive continued to seek escape, and he looked in to Václav's eyes. The young duke pitied him.

Václav asked of Grandmother Ludmila, "Will you buy that child for me?" She assented and sent her young servant to approach one trader named Jakob. He and Grandmother had long known and respected each other. The servant carried some cloth squares of value Grandmother had given him. He handed one to Jakob with words from his mistress, and the purchase was made.

The other sons and daughters of former free peasants were now destined to live lives of service in distant palaces of kings.

They brought the purchased child to the castle, and Václav insisted he dine with them.

His name was Podiven, and he had never been in such a place: a house with more than one room, with candles and lamps, and a table meant only for eating. His language was rustic, and he had many different words and queer phrasing, but he could speak to be understood. In a nervous release of emotion he did speak.

He told of his village, named Dobra Wioska, "Good Village Home," across mountains to the east, where his family had worshipped in the religion of Perun with their village priest. Raiders had attacked the village a year earlier. The people ran into the woods seeking shelter beneath sacred oaks and holy linden trees. They planned to return to their burned farms and rebuild, and await the next raid. They were not warriors, but simple herders seeking to live in peace in the world capricious gods had given them.

These people were not happy with the state of affairs. They wanted some protection, so they petitioned their rustic priest to use his magic to keep them safe. The priest wanted desperately to help his people. He went into the forest and prayed. The holy man burnt offerings and inhaled fumes of burning hemp. He brewed potions of henbane and belladonna, or whatever herbs those priests use to enter into the state where they can speak with gods.

Into the night he prayed and chanted and chewed henbane until he swooned. The priest experienced dreams, and his dreams told him what he must do. He traveled for most of a day to a town farther upriver, where he had a craftsman create amulets of lead and place in each a chip of a dark crystal. He brought them back to the village of Good Home.

The priest built a great fire in the holy place near the settlement and he spoke. He gave each household an amulet to hang over the threshold of their huts. Beneath each family's threshold they buried a bitch with one of her puppies to represent continuation of life. The priest sang a hymn to Perun and assured the village each household so prepared would never suffer an enemy carrying a blade across the threshold. He told them to continue their sacrifices and prayers to the gods.

A few months later, raiders from a Magyar tribe rode their ponies into the village, and though the Magyars expected combat, each household withdrew into its hut and waited for the warriors to withdraw.

But they did not withdraw.

From house to house, the Magyars burst in and crossed the threshold with their swords. Men, old women and babies were killed. They raped young girls and fertile women, and then the females and young boys were bound and led to their camp. After two days, they came to Prague. So, Václav and Ludmila found Podiven and saved him from mutilating surgery and death—or if he was lucky, a vapid and wasted life.

The girls and young lost women—including the mother and sisters of Podiven—were sold into their own form of bondage and carried away to far lands.

You are young Kristián, and I know you have heard some of the world's cruelty. There are always fresh horrors that will surprise you. They will throughout your life.

Our priest Dušan bought two older surviving boys of the burned village of Good Home, one with reddish hair and a single black eyebrow across his forehead. They were fed and taken to labor in the town's iron works east of the city. It is hard and dangerous work, and many workers there do not live long, though some do.

Václav asked Podiven if he had heard the message of Jesus or knew anything of Christianity. The child was ignorant, so Václav, under the approving watch of Grandmother Ludmila, told him of Jesus, quoting, "Let the little children come to me, and do not hinder them, for the kingdom of heaven belongs to such as these." He shared the Word with him, and told him the sorcery of pagan priests meant nothing, as was proven in the house of Podiven's own father.

Podiven had seen what putting faith in amulets of pagan gods could lead to. So, he accepted the teachings of Christ the Savior from the mouths of his own personal saviors and became wholly Christian. He was baptized and dedicated his young life to serve Ludmila and to her grandson Václav, and to their faith.

Podiven grew to be a strong young man, taller than most, the loyal page of Václav. Later in his life, he traveled with him and helped him in his missions. He served his lord even after Václav's death, as I will tell you later.

So, Václav with his servant Podiven went away to his education, accompanied by a learned priest and two of the duke's men-at-arms. They went to Budeč to learn the ways of the world and those of heaven.

I would not see him again for more than three years.

I stayed with Mother. And Mother had plans.

Father stood and told me that was the end of the night's history. He called a serving man to take me back down the dark hall to my room.

An elderly servant lighted my way to my chamber, next to my older brother's. It was about four paces long, about three wide, stone walls, with rushes on the floor and a platform cradling a straw-stuffed mat. The room was dark of course, but the servant lit a candle on a small shelf. I now had enough light to practice reading some Beatitudes after my prayers. I was still learning my Latin letters, though I could read them in Slavonic quite well by then. Latin letters are replacing Cyril's Slavonic alphabet in Bohemia.

Whenever I prayed, I always ended beseeching God to love Father and grant him mercy. I've been taught to do it since I could speak, and in the next days at Hrad Prague, Father told me why.

I lay down, and before I closed my eyes, I heard the door to my chamber latch from the outside.

I was locked in the room.

I had no fear of enemies there. If Father had enemies, I expected they would make a lot of noise before I was in any danger, and the house was full of his servants and retainers. Father's page Tira, even at his age, looked like a worthy fighter and would defend his duke well, and there were other men within the castle walls.

Perhaps someone might think of me as a threat? I was twelve years old and not to my full height yet. My traveling companions were sleeping, separate from me. Strong and armed as the two men were, there were many more serving the duke in his home.

Father told me something of the brutality of our world that night, and would tell me more in the coming days. But I believed the influence of the Church and the words of Jesus would temper the cruelty of mankind.

At least I did at the time.

So I lay inside my dark locked chamber, bundled against the cold. I was tired from my travels and Father's histories. I slept, and escaped from tales of burning villages and mutilated boys.

***

The next morning, I awakened at the sound of the latch being lifted from my door. A serving woman carrying a candle on her tray brought me cheese, bread with honey, fruit, and warm, watered wine.

She was an older woman, probably more than three decades old, and used to palace service. Her long hair was graying in streaks, and she wore a simple kitchen dress and apron, not fine clothing like Father's or my brother's, or even Tira's. No doubt she had her own history to tell, perhaps serving visitors in this very room in several ways, though I did not ask and she did not volunteer.

I mentioned to her the latch, and she nodded. She said, "Your brother, young Boleslav, he knows your father's story and is not taking risks." I had not yet heard the tale of how a younger brother might behave to a duke's heir.

When I finished eating, Tira came to the door and told me my father would see me when he was done with his council, before noon.

Tira was a serious man, lean and quiet. He wore a dirk at all times, and I noticed a chain vest beneath his tunic that bore the mark of a duke's page.

So I cleaned myself and prayed, then went to his hall's entrance. I waited until Father sent away his men. He waved me to my chair of last night, and the little dog Mazel sniffed my hand. He jumped into my lap, giving us both some warmth in the drafty room.

The duke took up his story where he left it the night before.

CHAPTER 2
Březen—A Time of Anticipation

While my brother Václav was away and our father was at the wars, and Grandmother was at Tetín or traveling and sharing new ways of farming, I stayed with Mother. She brought me deeper into the old religion.

Mother took me to the holy glades of wildflowers and grass where we worshipped Svantovít—the most powerful of the old gods—and Veles, god of cattle and wealth. We also worshipped Morana, the goddess of springtime, growth and harvest, and of death.

Our priest Dušan led us in singing hymns to our gods. We prayed to them for better crops, to cure illness, for easy births for the women, or victory in battle when we were at war. We shared mead, and sometimes a visiting fortune teller or oracle would inhale smoke from a holy fire and become entranced. He would mumble or scream in strange languages or toss bones on the ground to see how they laid, and what the gods foretold of our futures.

At the winter festival of Koleda, we sang songs of awakening light, of when the sun began to rise again to shine on our lands. Young people would wear costumes and go through the town singing songs. We built a bonfire of a huge tree log at sundown, and throughout the cold night we gathered around it. We heard tales of the gods, of Veles, Svantovít, Velká Matka Země the Earth Mother, and many other gods, and of wood spirits and water maidens, both good and evil.

But I learned not all evil comes from unknown spirits who hide in the forests. Some comes from people who are quite visible.

Our priest Dušan spoke of signs he had witnessed, shapes of clouds, songs of birds, figures he could see in the embers of fires and other ways the gods speak to men, and how he interpreted them. He built a story of what the omens might mean, and how we could order our lives to live in harmony with what Veles or other gods wanted, or how to avoid their wrath of disease or famine. He had knowledge of dealing with the gods, herbs, the winds, and many other things.

The priest's normal duties were, beyond harvesting his crops of honey and oats, to bless activities and events of the people. He prayed for birthing women, blessed new swords when they were given to officials, prayed over sick children and adults. When he attended to a sick person he chanted holy words, and sometimes played a small wooden flute to bring the power of healing from the goddess Živa.

He gave amulets of stone, or of wood and herbs for comfort, and to guard against disease and curses. He was often paid in a measure of grain or a quarter of lamb.

Dušan would bless new houses. When houses were built, men dug a square pit into the ground with post holes for the entranceway. Beneath these posts, the priest placed a sacrifice, a gift to the gods of fruit or grain, or, if the family was important, a chicken. For the most important families the priest butchered a pig and laid it beneath the doorpost, or even the head of a horse if the home builder was an important warrior.

Once I saw a different priest place something else.

Dušan's greatest power was counseling those who lost a loved one, or who were making a decision effecting a family's life. I think he was born with this power, and it is real.

At some events such as the midsummer festival of Koupel, after the feasting we built a large fire. In the darkness people jumped across the fire, and men and women would pair off and leave to love each other beneath the sacred trees, all with the blessing of the gods. In the morning the people bathed in the river, and in the weeks to come, if any of the women showed that they were to become mothers, husbands living in other villages and towns would be found for the women, and they began their family lives.

The priest Dušan was also in charge of the iron works, which alone made him the most important man in our land, save the duke himself.

He often had an apprentice or his shaggy dog with him. On a braided thong around Dušan's neck he wore an amulet of a powerful stone—a smoky, dark green crystal he told me fell from the sky. It was a healing gem said to protect him from disease and hurt. Since he also managed the drawing of iron from the earth, he needed to keep himself safe for the good of the country. He held secrets of smelting good iron and making steel.

Smelting lesser metals is not as difficult as working iron. Tin, lead, silver, copper, gold can all be refined from the earth, melted over a hot fire. Iron is less compliant. It demands more than a very hot fire: making iron takes great physical strength and exact timing, and an eye to the perfect mixture of carbon and ore at the exact heat, and the great work of muscles of men. Iron—both its creation and its possession—makes men strong.

The technique of iron making is very important for a country. The kingdom with good iron has good weapons, an advantage over enemies with lesser metal. Good iron helps the very survival of a nation. So, Dušan's work at the forge was deadly serious, though his religious services were mostly just joyful and happy.

But bad things can happen too, Kristián.

Here in Prague, Mother worked to lead me farther away from Grandmother's Christian religion, and she drew some of the town's people away, too.

While Václav was away at school, Mother sent for another priest. He called himself Veshtak, and fancied himself a thaumaturge, or "wonder worker." She knew him from her father's tribe, and he ranged over many lands to the east and the south. Some said he was originally from the land of Albanians, or perhaps from the Russians or Serbs. His name meant "quick-witted," or "clever," "expert." Some said it could be interpreted as "poison." He was thin and wiry, dark-haired, with a broad face and a black beard brushed to frame his face like a lion's mane.

Our local priest, Dušan, sheared his beard short for safety when working at the ironworks.

Veshtak traveled about to many towns and villages. I saw him again after Father died. Veshtak brought with him two men from Mother's tribe. One was of medium height and of a commanding nature named Tunna, who always carried a long dirk or stiletto as well as a sword. Tunna had two sons about the age of Václav. The other was Gomon, a very large man who armed himself with a mace—a war hammer. They both moved to Prague and lived there for years, and later near the castle I was to build to the east.

Years before, Veshtak had brought a young nursemaid slave for Mother. She was a gift from her father and was taken in a raid by Mother's tribe against the Saxons. She was called Saskia.

When Václav was born, Mother nursed him herself and weaned him as quickly as possible.

But Mother had Saskia nurse me soon after I was born, so mother need not be bothered with having to keep me near.

As I grew, Saskia taught me learning games and rhymes and songs in her German tongue. She was my wetnurse from my infancy to… later.

I sometimes wonder how my brother could take milk from a woman like Mother, yet become such an example of love and justice.

***

I was only seven, and was being schooled differently than Václav. Mother discouraged my study of letters and the Bible. She told me to spend more time learning methods of sword and spear, and riding under Veshtak's men-at-arms. Some local boys my age joined me in lessons. One was the son of a prominent shepherd, and for years he was my closest friend, really up until your birth.

My training had little to do with texts. I learned to sign my name, of course.

I was well practiced in arms. By the time I was eight I could wield a small axe and a spear, and I practiced with small wooden swords. Tunna's sons practiced with me and with my best friend, Hněvsa. They taught me one special move, to draw my sword from its sheath and, in the same smooth motion, strike the neck of my battle practice dummy.

In Budeč, Václav progressed in his studies, learning Latin as well as improving his Greek letters and basics of ruling a growing nation. He also continued his training in arms and became proficient with sword, mace and horse as befits a duke who must lead men in battle. But he preferred studying the Holy Texts.

***

Father and Mother were often at odds, and Father seemed unhappy when they were together. He stayed away at the wars, and finally we learned he died.

A courier came to our castle and told us there had been a battle. Proud Father, with his sword named "Kousat," or "Bite," and wearing plates of armor, was attacked by a determined swarm of axe men apparently trained for this purpose.

The duke and seventy of his horsemen had gained an advantage in a battle against a tribe of Hungarians who had been raiding our borders. At the end of a day of fighting, the Czechs were resting their spears on the ground near the top of a small hill as the sun set.

Suddenly, a party of enemy archers on foot crested the hill above them, and shot their arrows at Father's men, some who had removed their helmets. The men were stunned. Some were killed, and many of their horses startled and ran off.

The Czechs leapt to their weapons as several staggered and fell from arrows. The remaining knights and men gathered into formation to charge the eighty paces to the archers. As they organized to move up the hill, nine grim and determined axe men, lightly armored, quietly ran from hiding in a nearby copse of trees. They ran from behind to the center of the line unnoticed by the Czechs, who in the dim light were still being accurately targeted.

The assassins swung their long-handled axes in a sudden attack in the darkening air from an unexpected quarter and clove the heads and shoulders of the duke and his pages.

When they saw the duke killed, the axe men quickly retreated, but not before Czech horsemen pursued and killed several.

So, Father was dead and Václav was the new duke, but he was too young.

***

Emissaries from the Frankish kingdom and the halls of the Moravian king conferred with Grandmother Ludmila and with my mother, Dragomira. They decided Mother and Grandmother would rule as regents until Václav came of age. Václav was twelve, and I was only nine. He was too young to rule, but he was old enough to be designated heir with the haircutting ceremony.

Ceremonial cutting the hair of a prince symbolizes his passing into adulthood and taking up the tools and weapons of a young man. Haircutting could also mean tonsuring, as the heads of Christian monks are, to bring them closer to God. Some of Dragomira's friends suggested Václav, with his peaceful and unaggressive ways, should become a monk instead of duke. The power over the Czechs could stay in the hands of Grandmother, and of Mother, whose strong nature was more suited to command.

Mother had ruled while Father was at the wars, and she could direct men. She relished that power. She was taller than most women and showed determination when she gave orders.

But women do not rule Czechs, not since the ancient story of Libuše, daughter of the leader Krok. When that ancient ancestor of ours died, Libuše ruled wisely, but some men criticized her judgements, blaming her gender. So, she married Přemysl and made the Plowman our leader, founder of our dynasty. Only men have ruled our people ever since.

Ludmila and Dragomira could never rule other than as regents. When Václav reached age, he would rule.

The haircut of princes is distinctive and is limited to noble classes.

His head was shaved to about a thumb's length above the ears and all about the back, so he appears to be wearing a hat or helmet cap of hair.

Václav was really too young for the ceremony, but it was agreed he would have his hair cut to symbolize his right to rule when he was older. He was shorn in ceremony, and Grandmother's Christian priest Paul made a speech, proclaiming to the assembled boyars and prominent townspeople that he is heir to the ducal throne, and he would be their new leader when he achieved enough age.

He was shown the farmer's boots of our ancestor, Přemysl the Plowman. They showed every ruler the boots to reinforce that though he rules, he is the descendant of a common man, as was his farmer ancestor.

They gave Václav weapons. Dušan's bladesmiths had long prepared the sword Václav would bear, and would wield in battle if necessary. It was long and broad, made of Dušan's good Czech iron and steel, a triumph of the armorer's craft.

Dušan and his smiths had forged and crafted armor for stout pauldrons to protect his shoulders, and a helmet, to protect him from blows from above, such as those that killed our father.

The helmet was shiny steel. At Grandmother Ludmila's order it was set with a relief crucifix of inlaid silver on the decorative browband and nose guard. About its base hung an aventail of fine chain mail to protect his neck. It was a beautiful example of the finest work of Dušan's craftsmen.

Václav named the sword, "Obránce Víry," meaning "Faith's Defender."

The young duke was large for his age, though not yet full-grown. These weapons and armor were not given to him yet, but displayed to show the arms he would bear when he reached his maturity in four years and would become duke.

Hněvsa and Tunna's older son, Tuza, stood near me. Tuza whispered, "He will make a poor leader. You should sit on that throne, Boleslav. You will be strong." Hněvsa agreed.

It is a heady experience to have strong men older than you telling you that you will be a great ruler—greater than your brother. Well, I remained silent.

Oh, Kristián, I think the dog you're holding might need to go outside. Take Mazel for a short walk. I have more to tell you.

***

Václav stayed with Mother and me for half a year.

During that time Grandmother visited from Hrad Tetín. She spent hours continuing to teach Václav and me the Christian ways she loved, though I had fallen behind in reading and just pretended, following their suggested leads in prayers. When Grandmother was not with us, Mother did not allow Christian prayers and studies, though Václav kept a book hidden in his clothes.

Mother tried to keep Christian priests from visiting Václav, but he found a way to see them. Later, after Grandmother died, Mother even told Tunna to cut down any priests who tried to see him.

She took us to some pagan celebrations, such as blessing waters of a spring when they killed a pig, and its blood was caught and passed around for the people to drink. Blood is good food and used in sauces and puddings, but Václav would not drink it in a pagan ritual.

He held to his faith despite Mother's wishes and kept his prayers secret from her.

Sometimes he recited rhyming Psalms to me, I guess to give me a chance to become more Christian. I still remember some of them. Some seem to tell his story, and maybe mine, too:
"The Lord the rod shall of thy strength
    send from out of Zion:
In the midst of thine enemies
    have thou dominion.
Willing thy folk in thy days' power,
    in holy beauties be:

From morning's womb thou hast the dew
    of thy youth unto thee.
The Lord who is at thy right hand,
    wounding shall strike through kings
In that same day wherein that he
    his indignation brings.
He shall among the heathen judge
    and fill with bodies dead
Great places and over many lands
    he shall strike them through the head."

My brother (my brother!) always tried to draw me to the ways of Christ. And his page Podiven knew his bible studies, too. Podiven taught the Gospels to willing servants in our house, and to his friend from his home village with the one eyebrow named Bratumil. His friend was now Dušan's blade apprentice.

Mother finally had Václav return to Budeč, where his tutor could continue his studies of Latin and Greek. She wished him gone so she could make her own plans.

And once more, it was years before I saw my brother again.

***

Mother and Grandmother did not get along well, proving the truism of mothers-in-law and the wives of their sons. I think their enmity was worse than most.

Grandmother Ludmila was mindful of her daughter-in-law's animosity, and stayed with her priest Paul, and with Mstena and other servants in her castle Tetín—all Christian and very devoted to her.

During this time, Mother Dragomira savored the taste of power. She plotted with Veshtak and his men Tunna and Gomon how she might rule forever.

Tunna was proud and strong, a natural leader. Gomon was a very large warrior, slow to speak, and had enormous strength. Gomon looked up to Tunna at that time, and followed his orders. These two became leaders of those who resisted the changes Ludmila was bringing to the people.

Veshtak was not in Prague much. He was always away on some quiet mission of Mother's, or perhaps her father's. But when he was here, Mother held private meetings with him and Tunna and Gomon.

The priest Veshtak and the men he brought with him found friends among those of our people who resisted the Christian teachings of Ludmila, including the father of my best friend, Hněvsa. These men did not want their religion to come through the hands of foreign-speaking Germans, yet their pagan faith under gentle Dušan was not inspired. They wanted something more moving, and Veshtak could excite a congregation.

Veshtak held ceremonies with more blood, where more cruel pagan rituals were practiced, rituals many of us had never seen.

I privately preferred Dušan's services to Veshtak's. The meetings led by Dušan were often in the morning, with mist rising from the land and sunlight sparking from dewy fields where he spoke. His words were lively, and he told of sounds he heard in rippling streams, from wind in mountain forests, and then he created a story of what it could mean. The words that whisper among branches and leaves could guide our behavior for the good of our people, the forest, and the city.

Dušan's manner was gentle, and he usually smiled. When not in a service, he dressed in a close-fitting tunic and long trousers, and this facilitated his work at the smelter. He wore a woolen robe during services. He carried a pouch strapped across his shoulder, which often carried food and some tools of his work, or herbs and amulets. His hound Král was often with him, a bushy-coated shepherd, and he had an apprentice—a tall, large-boned young woman with long straw-colored hair, learning the lore of herbs.

Dušan could read patterns in clouds and hear from birdsong the gods' will.

Once Dušan drew a dove from his pouch as if by magic, then said a prayer and released it to the sky, carrying the good wishes of our people with it to the gods.

Veshtak's services were different, held mostly at twilight or deep night. He drew extreme emotions in firelight from the watchers, and his proclamations threatened punishments for people in the city who acted in ways he said were against the gods. He relished the effects his actions had on his congregation and used elements of his services to amaze and take power over the people. "Lord Svantovít, hear our prayer!"

He performed blood sacrifices more often than Dušan had ever done. Mother took me to watch a live piglet struggling as it was slowly strangled, or a trusting dog cut open while still alive as Veshtak read the future in his throbbing organs. This sort of thing hardens a person's sensibilities, and the congregation began to expect such a ceremony— and some even more extreme.

I should mention here, pagan priests are not the only priests who mislead their congregations. Beware of any church leader using fear and threats to gain power over the people. They are among us, and probably always will be.

Veshtak charged those who spoke against his practices with evil possession, as if they were under a spell. He said they must be cleansed through trials of pain or denial, such as wearing a sharp stone in their shoe, or forbidding them to eat anything but raw oats for weeks at a time.

Veshtak had the power of the curse.

Mother's priest always dressed in loose clothes, long tunics and robes, with what I later learned had hidden pockets and pouches. Veshtak's stone amulet was red, a carnelian set in lead, with runes worked into metal about the crystal. Veshtak kept a quiet demeanor and did not show emotion when not at a service. He was usually silent around me. He always spoke in low tones to Mother and to his men, Tunna, and the large one, Gomon.

Tunna and Gomon were rarely apart. These "knights" always dressed in battle tunics and maintained a military air about them. They seemed under orders of Veshtak. He sent them on missions to bring him materials he needed or word of a movement of raiding parties or of certain people.

Our house had a meeting room, and sleeping chambers for Mother and another for me and Václav when he was there. There were servants' rooms too, for Saskia and the others. A slave and a guard slept outside the door of Mother's room, the guard on a pallet and the slave on a rug.

I had the castle rebuilt later into the stone building we're in now, but then there were outbuildings such as the granary where we stored shelves of turnips, beets and other roots, and jars of oats and millet and smoked meat. Other buildings nearby were the mead house, the armory, and the stable. My grandfather built a small chapel when he became Christian, and some townspeople used it when the Christian priest was in town. He would only come when the dowager, my grandmother came—rarely since Father died.

Anyway, Mother, Veshtak, and the others gathered in the granary for their private meetings.

Once I saw the men bring Veshtak a cloth sack he peered into, then smiled, nodded and put it away. When he was gone, I crept into his chamber and looked into the bag. In it was the grinning head of a man. I don't know who it was.

Oh, yes, Kristián, this shook me, too. Our world holds terrors.

***

Tunna and Gomon became my trainers, as were Tunna's two sons. Tuza was seven years older than I, and Tira four years my senior. I fought them in practice bouts with wooden swords. I learned their ways of fighting, which gave no quarter and used whatever methods would win. Neither of them ever put out my eye or broke anything more than a finger bone of mine. They had a potent influence on me. They kept it until the night of your birth.

Tuza, being older, was the natural leader of the three of us.

He seemed always angry about not being born into nobility, not being in line for a royal position. I think he held it against Václav, heir to the throne of Bohemia.

In spring and summer the three of us would follow trails in the forest to remote homes of peasants, and we took bread and honey from them. If they argued, Tira and Tuza showed them their weapons, and they were quiet.

Tuza had a new beard and was fully grown. He had an air of command about him, like his father. He told me I was the duke's son, and it wasn't stealing to take peasants' food without it being offered because everything in the land was owned by the duke. I had not heard this from anyone before, but Tira went along with everything Tuza said, and being so young, so did I.

At one home, Tuza forcibly kissed the couple's daughter. He returned to us with a heady smile, and we rode off.

I was still too young to like girls, though they told me I would someday, and they were right.

Father stood and told me he must walk about to loosen his limbs. He called a servant and ordered food for me. Father and Tira walked out of the hrad into town. From the bright, cold sunshine of winter they entered a building to meet with some businessmen.

I went to the stables and spoke with my groom. He and my servant had slept in a barracks next to the stable. They had fed well and enjoyed the company of the duke's groomsmen. They told me some of the men were watchful overnight and did not sleep. No one was unfriendly, but they appeared alert and cautious, which I suppose is not a bad thing for the duke's men. Even if my men were servants of the duke's family, they were strangers there.

I walked to St. George's Basilica and entered. The building was stone, with ornate wood carvings. Candles burned at the altar, and a monk knelt in prayer at the tomb of my great-grandmother. Here lay Ludmila, "Christ's Handmaiden," as my father told me.

The husband of Ludmila, Duke Bořivoj, began the building of the church. Its construction continued after a pause, when Father's brother Václav completed it and had it consecrated.

They built a choiry into the sanctuary. Separate quarters for nuns and for monks were part of the structures surrounding the building. Monks took turns praying for Ludmila and sent constant prayers to God, so he might know how we Czechs praise Him and our beloved saint and that we thank Him for sending her to us. I was told when Ludmila died her body was brought here and laid in this holy place, in the arms of Christ.

That afternoon, Father told me how she died.

I knelt and said a prayer for my great-grandmother Ludmila, and for our nation. I closed with another prayer, asking God to forgive my father for a sin I had not yet learned.

I thanked the monks for their constancy. They seemed grateful I had spoken to them, but at twelve years of age, I had little of the knowledge and sanctity they must have had.

I stepped out into the cold glare as my older brother and some of his companions rode by. He looked princely in his cape and hat, and handled his horse as masterfully as he must someday control his people's fate. He gave me a brief nod and smile, but his fellows looked at me sternly.

As much as Prague is a wonderful city, home of my father and seat of Bohemian power, I was eager to leave it and enter the world of study and prayer in the land of the Franks.

When I entered the castle again, a servant took me to where Father had again seated himself by the fire. His little dog looked at him adoringly as he stroked its ears.

"It is time to get on with the tale," said Father. "You will leave Bohemia. You must learn of my great sin, and find me a way into that Land of Goodness, where I may see Grandmother Ludmila once more. And my brother!" He turned to the fire and composed himself, then began again.

Grandmother Ludmila persisted in her plans to improve the lands and continually sought ways to help our people. Her work was long-lasting and benefitted the country, probably forever. She brought new types of grapes, grains, and cattle to the land, and sought better types of other crops.

And she loved her people.

She established churches and installed priests with words of blessing, and directed them to tend their human flocks and to help care for needs of the poor and helpless.

She traveled the land and planted orchards of plum, cherry, and apple in many villages, always praising Christ. She converted many people through the simple example of her piety and good works.

She spent her days in service and prayer as befitted "Christ's Handmaid." In the evening, she always went to a chapel or a chamber of her home to end the day in thanksgiving and prayer to God, the father of Jesus the Christ.

Once in my tenth year, after my father had died and Mother and Grandmother Ludmila ruled our land, Mother took me to a pagan service in the glade in a holy grove of oaks, during the harvest festival of Dožínky. This was the second afternoon of the festival, after the previous night's bonfire and the massive kolo dance and carnal frolicking of people afterwards, and the morning bathing. Václav was away in Budeč.

Some workers from the iron forges played drums at the eastern edge of the glade, and there was a constant throbbing in the air. Our priest Dušan had built a large fire, and it illuminated the small forest field in fading sunlight. The men and women of our community had baked a round honey cake so large that Dušan could hide behind it, and this portended a good harvest for the coming year.

Dušan's apprentice was a very tall woman, about twenty years old, adept at brewing teas of forest herbs for settling a sour stomach and making poultices for healing cuts. The novice could also translate shapes made when she poured wax into cool water, which is one way the gods told us their wishes. She was learning the ways of birds and beasts from Dušan. She dressed in a gray cloak, and all expected her to become a great priestess herself.

At Mother's suggestion, Dušan had sent for an oracle from a land to the east, from the heart of Old Moravia. Our family party was just me, Mother and her body slave, and my milk sister Saskia. We joined other worshippers at twilight near trees where the bonfire was already burning. Dušan was speaking to the oracle, and his black and brown hound was alert, lying at the gathering's edge.

The priest Veshtak and his men Tunna and Gomon did not attend, nor Tunna's sons.

Dušan and Veshtak did not get on well, despite praying to mostly the same gods.

The oracle suggested by Mother was about thirty years old, though still young-looking. She had bright red hair, and she dressed in an enormous white hooded robe. Her assistant was a young boy who placed oil lamps in a circle around her. Dušan told the fifty or so people at the gathering that the woman was a famous seer who could predict crops, wars, weather, and the future of our country now that our king was dead. I also think he hoped to draw some of our religious pagans away from the harsher type of religion Veshtak taught.

The woman seer had shaved brows and very pale skin, nearly like milk, nearly transparent. She began a series of chants as she lit a large lamp and drew forth dried mushrooms from a pouch under her cloak. She began chewing them. The drums played a cycle of nine beats. They repeated this nine times, then began the pattern again.

We danced the Kolo circle again, all of us grasping hands and stepping around the clearing in a great arc. Dušan led us in song, and it was thrilling as we danced faster to music of the drums and flutes and fanfrnochs. The oracle drew herself more into a trance.

After the ninth round of the drum cycle the oracle put a bundle of cut plants on a small charcoal brazier, and she inhaled their smoke. The fumes she breathed in seemed to stagger her, and she began sweating and shaking. Her eyes became bright and flickered about.

She spoke with grunts, and we knew she was going to predict our future, what would become of us. Her servant boy Kamil was always by her side. She pointed to a dish, and he brought it to her. She drank from it.

The oracle stepped from the circle of lamps and walked to the center of the grassy glade lit by the great fire. She began to turn. She spun and whispered unknown words. The oracle reeled about the glade speaking her strange chants, turning faster in a widening circle. Her white robe spun from her in a wide, moving blur in the moonlight. I glimpsed a red stone on a cord around her neck, like the carnelian of Veshtak.

She stopped suddenly and looked at each of our faces in silence. Her eye rested on a black shawl on one woman, and she pointed to it. Kamil brought it to her and she put it over her head, in the manner of a Christian woman in prayer. She began speaking again, in a rhyming chant of wordless sounds as she stepped one way, then another. She flung the shawl from her head into the fire. The oracle distorted her face into a dreadful mask of bulging eyes and lolling tongue.

The crackling bonfire, the throbbing drums, and the gasps of the soothsayer were the only sounds.

She pointed to a cudgel a man had brought. Her child servant brought it to her. The seer turned it over and over, examining it as if it were a magic object, then swung it around her head, faster and faster. Things happened quickly.

The oracle screamed and flew at the priest, shrieking the whole time. She swung at him, striking Dušan a strong blow on the shoulder and knocking him to the ground. His dog, Král, barked and rushed to his master, lying in the grass. The slave youth Bratumil from the ironworks ran to him. Dušan's woman apprentice came to his aid, and as she bent over him, the oracle struck her head. The blow killed her. It was surprising to see such fury and strength from the woman.

She flew at some nobles, and their pages defended their lords and finally struck down the witch with their long daggers. They dragged her body, still twitching, to the bonfire and heaved her upon it. Her hair sizzled and flamed as her face turned to me, eyes wide. She sneered as she burned to death.

That sight has stayed with me ever since.

As her young servant boy Kamil protested, the men grasped him to throw on the flaming logs. It was pitiful to see the child in such fear.

Dušan regained himself, and with Král and Bratumil by his side, he held them from the murder of the boy. After a moment, the priest took a deep breath, then spoke loudly, "That oracle was a demon. She fooled me into thinking she was a seer. Now she is destroyed. Let that be enough!"

He steadied himself, aided by the young slave from the forge, and he sprinkled mead and water from the sacred spring about the clearing. He chanted to the goddess Morana to cleanse the site and make it holy again.

His apprentice had been young, still with years of learning and healing ahead of her. She had already gained expert knowledge of herbs and medicinal roots, all the healing arts, now lost in an instant.

At the direction of Dušan, men carried the body of his assistant to the other side of the dale and laid her on a pallet away from the light from the bonfire, in the cool glow of moonlight. He bade his dog to sit and guard.

Many were still in shock from the sudden attack and began drifting away into the night. I saw one man secretly cross himself.

Dušan uncapped a gourd bottle and poured a gentle drop of oil over his dead apprentice's brow. He continued to chant as he massaged it into her cooling skin. He put a lamp at her head, and another at her feet, and stood over her with many blessing prayers. Later, when the fire had burned low, he would commit her to the flames in a private ceremony.

I think he cared deeply for her.

Mother directed Saskia to bring me home while she stayed with the priest and some of his slaves. "See that he is well fed," she told her.

"Your own milk." Mother was still having Saskia nurse me, though not often anymore.

Saskia would never disobey Mother. Any resistance had long since been beaten from her.

Nursing from Saskia had begun to feel different from simple nourishment from her body. When you are old enough to have a conversation with the woman who is breastfeeding you, it is, well, different. Mother knew this, knew the maturing nine-year-old boy she was training as I moved toward adulthood.

Saskia looked at me with a sad and hopeless face as we walked back to the city.

Dušan took the oracle's servant boy Kamil into his care, and he eventually became Dušan's assistant and apprentice.

Later, I learned why Tunna and Gomon weren't at the pagan meeting. They missed the mad oracle's death, but I learned they were present at another.

Saskia and I walked back to the palace. The lamp she carried shot flickering beams and shadows about us.

She was silent, and then she quietly sobbed and whimpered.

I asked her what was wrong.

"My life has been so changed," she told me.

What did she mean?

When she had composed herself, she told me, in her German accent. "It was mid-spring, with a clear sky and fields of flowers. A clean breeze carried the songs of birds in their mating dances. Then came a battle, and the Wends defeated my father's people. They killed my father. Their fighters invaded the village where we lived. They killed all our men, including my handsome young man who gave me my baby. He was so beautiful and strong, but they overcame him. Our child was only three months old, and the Wendish warriors had no use for babies. They only wanted us women and young girls."

We walked silently.

"Didn't they have their own women?" I asked.

Saskia didn't answer.

We reached the house and went to my room.

Finally, she said, "They took away all the boys and sold them, or forced them into their army. When they were done with us women, they brought us back to their town and distributed us among the people there as house servants or nursemaids. My body still had milk for my baby."

Saskia removed her top clothes and I could see fresh whip scars. She brought my face to her body.

"What happened to your baby?" I asked, as I started nursing.

"They killed him," she said. "They killed him."

So, Saskia had become my wet-nurse for the benefit of my mother, who wanted to return to a more independent life.

She put her hand on the back of my head and stroked me as I suckled, and sang a quiet Frankish lullaby I couldn't understand.

I drank milk from her body that should have been her son's.

CHAPTER 3
Listopad—The Time of Falling Leaves

Two days after Dušan's apprentice and the oracle died, word came to me that Grandmother's servant Mstena was back in Prague and wished to see me.

He bore a dreadful tale.

On the night of Dušan's service, men had visited Grandmother Ludmila at Hrad Tetín.

This is the castle Václav had visited as an infant fourteen years earlier.

But that evening, a raiding party of armed men rode to Tetín. They broke into the castle and overpowered the servants. Ludmila was at her evening prayers.

Grandmother prayed at the altar that St. Methodius had once blessed, and where lay a copy of scriptures in his own hand. Candles and lamps lit the peaceful small chamber. She held a prayer shawl over her head as she chanted prayers to Christ.

"Lord, hear my prayer!"

Her servant Mstena was there in his own prayerful reverie, though not at the altar.

The assassins opened the door. Grandmother knew her time was at hand. She prayed in earnest tones as she realized she was about to be brought to meet Jesus Himself.

Mstena told me she said, "If you must kill me, use a blade that I might die like the martyrs." Many Christian martyrs have been beheaded or stabbed with spears or shot with arrows, all bloody deaths.

These killers had no desire to give her a last wish.

One of her assassins pulled the prayer shawl from her hair. The servant Mstena screamed and charged to save his mistress. One of them, a large man, put out an arm and stopped him. As Mstena wrestled his way from the man's grasp, the leader twisted the shawl around the throat of my grandmother. He tightened it and pulled the prayer shawl to choke the life from her. At the altar of the Prince of Peace, Grandmother's last words were praises to God.

Mstena pushed his way free and escaped to the woods, shouting, "Murder! Sacrilege!"

Armed men who had accompanied the murderers sacked the castle, and the remaining servants and guards fled to the forest. Ludmila's priest was found hidden in his chambers and was stabbed to death on the spot.

Then the murderers rode away.

The castle household, those not killed, would lament for months.

Mstena made his way secretly to our home. He avoided Mother, Veshtak, and their men, who did not like him. He told me his tale, and I remembered the mad oracle woman who placed a shawl over her head as if in prayer, just as Grandmother was being murdered at that very instant. So perhaps the seer had some talent for prophecy.

Or perhaps she was aware of a plan.

I recalled the carnelian crystal around her neck, similar to the larger one Veshtak wore. Had she killed Dušan that night, there would be no power in our land to challenge Mother, who now alone ruled Bohemia as the Regent Dragomira.

In our chambers Mstena was agitated. He constantly looked around as if fearful of being discovered by someone, and I suppose if the killers found him, he might indeed have cause to worry. I suggested he should go to Budeč and find Václav.

He had already planned to do this, and had some traveling funds. He felt he should stop here before he went to alert Dušan. But he said he saw Veshtak in the town and decided to leave immediately after telling me.

"You must tell Dušan about the murder," he said. The murder of my sweet grandmother, now gone forever.

The next day, I sought out Dušan. He and his new apprentice Kamil were at work at the charcoal pits. As I approached Dušan's dog, Král barked a warning.

One worker was a large, strong young man, with a single eyebrow across his head and reddish hair. I recognized Bratumil, who Václav had described, a slave from the village where Podiven was captured. He had become a valuable worker for Dušan, learning his craft of iron—blades, tools, weapons—at the iron smeltery.

Smelting iron requires a large amount of charcoal. Making charcoal is a simple process, but requires exact timing to get the best results. Dušan was schooling Kamil in counting steps as they walked around the furnaces to measure time. So many circuits measured the time to add more fuel, or to open a vent, or to smother the fire—all to bake wood into charcoal.

As I approached them, Dušan smiled at me.

Dušan had a talent, a natural ability to make you feel you were the entire world. This can't be taught. It is born into a very few special people, and is a great power but can be misused. Kristián, perhaps you have met someone like this. If not, someday you may.

Dušan saw I was distraught. He placed his hand on my shoulder and led me to a bench near the huge covered pits. Here was a tally board for the number of circuits he and Kamil had walked around the charcoalliery. He moved the tablet, and we sat in the shade of one of few trees still standing in this area. Kamil continued counting circuits around the fire pits, chanting his prayers, or memorizing ways of divination or some other obscure talent.

I told Dušan of the murder, and that Mstena said I should warn him of his danger.

Dušan continued to smile and let me know he had already heard of the crime and of his threatened situation. He said the murder of the Christian dowager, my grandmother, was a heinous offense, even if she was not of his faith.

"Do not worry about me, Prince Boleslav," he said, and told me he had prepared precautions for his own safety. He had sent word to Václav of events here and at Tetín.

I saw some of his slaves were armed with dirks, and two men from town were also lounging about the edge of the clearing with swords near their hands. He said, "As you see, I also have some small measure of power."

That left me to wonder of the powers of the wizard, and whether his good powers could contend with the fearsome and malevolent strength of Mother's priest, Veshtak.

The two sons of Tunna walked by the edge of the charcoalliery. They called to me to join them in the city.

He said, "Here, keep this close to your heart." The priest drew from his pouch a small polished crystal with a vein of gold within it, pierced and strung with a thin leather thong. He told me, "Amulets have no power by themselves, Boleslav. But this will remind you of good within you." He touched the vein in the crystal. "See the gold strand within the stone, and look for the good within yourself. There is some good within everyone."

Kristián, I want to believe this, but I do not.

Dušan said, "Amulets and tokens remind us of a feeling, a hope. View this when you need to reflect on yourself." And with his eyes on me, he handed me this token I show you now. Kristián, see the gold strand in the clear crystal? I have kept it near me and reflected on it ever since.

Then Dušan spoke low to me, "Best to keep our counsels to ourselves, young prince." So, the pagan priest and I became closer friends and shared a bond, not exactly secret, but not well known.

I left him for the company of my friends, Tunna's sons. I did not see him often again in private, though sometimes we shared counsel.

***

With the death of Ludmila, Dragomira was sole regent of Bohemia. She directed churches to be closed, or burned, and priests to be killed or driven from the land. Resentment grew between Christian believers and pagans.

The body of Ludmila was laid to rest at Tetín. The good works of her life created scores of followers. They began pilgrimages to her grave and left many gifts and burned candles. The reverent glow lit the night at her burial place.

After some weeks, after the time of falling leaves, it became clear to Mother that local people continued to honor Grandmother, even to call her saintly. Mother had her body exhumed and moved to the same church standing here in Prague, one of the few churches she had not destroyed. It was built by Ludmila's husband, and dedicated to St. George, so any honors or supposed miracles could be attributed to that saint rather than to Grandmother Ludmila.

***

Veshtak's pagan calls to his followers were very much in line with Mother's plans for stronger control over the Czechs. She continued to encourage me to witness Veshtak's sacrifices and services.

Once, late in the year, she brought me to a funeral service of a chief in a village a day's journey to the east. He had been a supporter of Mother's, and had named his son Dragomir after her.

When the chief died, Veshtak went to the village for the funeral and brought the people together in a field outside their settlement. His knights Tunna and Gomon and Tunna's sons Tuza and Tira accompanied him. They built a very large wood fire with more fuel set aside, and a feast with great quantities of food and drink. The chief's corpse was laid on a platform near the fire.

A chorus of women and then men voiced ancient hymns. Shepherd's bagpipes played, and throbbing drums filled the glade with rhythm.

This dead chief had four wives. The youngest was chosen to accompany him on his journey in death. She had not borne him any children. Perhaps the chief's age had made him past the time of siring children. The older three wives walked with her into the clearing.

Looking back on it now, I think they were jealous of her youthful beauty. They were much older, and mothers of his children.

As the sun fell, the three widows wailed in mourning. The younger wife, about sixteen years old, walked with them through the crowd in the dimming twilight. She wore a loose, long robe, and walked in a trance, having been fed herbs and medicines by the priest. A broad, open-mouthed smile was on her face. Her eyes glowed in a wide, staring gaze. The four women went forward and stood under the fire shadow of Veshtak. He spoke.

"We have lost our beloved leader, and we all mourn his passing! The sky darkens, the goddess Morana takes him into her arms! The very stones cry! See his women," and the four wives stood before him in the fire's light. "They moan at loss from his missing! They weep and wail, sad songs of their grief!" The three older women cried wordless screams. "One will accompany him on his journey." The young wife turned to him with an open-eyed smile.

All men looked closely at the woman, dressed in a light-colored sacrificial robe. They led her to a special skin hut near the pyre. At Veshtak's signal, his apprentice drew the robe from the young woman's shoulders, and light from the bonfire displayed her womanly form to the crowd.

"We who have loved the village chief will show our love by congress with this wife, who will so soon meet him in the next world."

The young girl shivered and her smile grew more broad, wild, like a mask of ecstasy and terror both at once, though I don't know if she even heard what was being said.

Veshtak took the young woman's hand and led her into the tent that was specially constructed for this event. His apprentice drew back the doorway, and inside was light from an oil lamp on the floor, where the dead chief's bed of bearskins and furs was laid out. Veshtak led the naked woman to the furs as the apprentice let fall the door curtains. Shadows played on walls of the tent as Veshtak loosened his clothes and sank to lie with the widow.

Mother turned her bright eyes to me, as if to share what these pagan ceremonies mean to men, and would mean to me when I grew into manhood. All I need do was to follow her words, leading me to the worship of old ways and gods.

After a time, Veshtak opened the tent drape, and he pointed to the new village chief Dragomir, who with eyes bulging eagerly unclasped his belt and went into the tent with the young drugged widow, as Veshtak exited.

I did not comprehend all the ceremony signified other than men bred with the woman. I was only a child, and as the evening progressed, music and fire and drums and pipes created an air of fantasy beyond anything I had yet seen. I will never forget that night.

As shepherd bagpipes screamed wild dirges, man after man entered the tent, then staggered out. Tunna and Gomon, Tuza and even young Tira, only fourteen, they all took their turns. Each man exiting the tent was handed a stoup of mead. Each man joined his fellows around a table bearing a large bowl of roasted horse flesh, which they ate from. They gathered by the displayed body of their dead chief, his spear and sword arrayed beside him.

They drank deep and shared stories of their chief, and perhaps of their night's experience with his doomed young widow.

The village was not large, and after about thirty men of the village and Veshtak's company had passed through the tent, Veshtak had the body and weapons of the leader brought from his display table to near the fire. They laid another pile of wood around the body, and they poured oil on it and on him. A brand from the large fire was laid on the fuel, and the fire grew into the night. They placed more wood over the chief.

We watched as the flame caught. Smoke and embers boiled into the sky, up to moon and stars, taking his soul to live forever with his fathers and their fathers long passed.

The young woman, again in her robe, was brought from the tent, no longer smiling but with wide, unseeing eyes, delirious now, still entranced by herbs and drink, and perhaps by the experience of the past few hours with Veshtak and all the village men.

The other wives brought her over to the burning body, and the men cast the robes and furs of their dead leader on the fire. Then in an instant they bound the young widow's wrists and ankles and lifted the dazed woman, and hurled her into the flames.

Despite her state of trance, she understood this was her death, and she screamed in pain in a horrid howl as they cast more oil upon her. She did not try to flee the flames, but remained on the fire, jerking and twitching about, all the while howling as the drums beat and the people sang a funeral song. My eyes could not turn from the gruesome sight. It was the second time I saw a woman burned before me.

That night seared into my memory with all the emotions a cruel pagan priest might wish. But at my age of eleven, I wondered why the woman was killed after she had bred with all those men. I knew the purpose of cow and horse and pig breeding was to produce offspring. Yet this newly bred woman was killed. It was shocking and made no sense to me.

It was just another mystery I pondered that night, and in nights and weeks and years to come.

As we grow older, mysteries multiply.

I see my tale has shaken your Christian sensibilities, Kristián. I can offer you no refuge from learning the ways of this world. We can pray for it in the next!

The hour was late, and Father bade me good night.

I was shaken by his tale of a custom of the old religion. I would seek peace in Holy Words before my candle cooled and sleep took me.

Again, the serving man lit my way down the hallway to my chamber. He told me my older brother was spending the next two nights at Hrad Boleslav, the castle Father had built twenty years earlier.

I'd visited there before. It was on a hill with a clear view of the Jizera River and far beyond. It would be a good place for a watchtower.

I made my evening prayers, pondered the Beatitudes I read the previous night, and how they could apply to what I learned of my father's grandmother, Ludmila.

"Blessed are the pure in heart,
for they will see God.
Blessed are those who are persecuted because of righteousness,
for theirs is the kingdom of heaven."

I slept with thoughts of her life on my mind. No one latched the door that night.

The next morning, the serving woman again gave me bread and honey, and again I met Father in his hall.

He was not easy in mind. I knew this day I would learn of the sin which tortured him so—so much that he would tell his most private thoughts to a child he barely knew, and who had always held him in great awe and reverence.

We stopped occasionally to eat and such, but I will write without interruption of this day's tale.

He spoke long, and I silently listened.

CHAPTER 4
Červen—The Time of Worms

The spring after I turned thirteen, Mother held a haircutting ceremony for me. She did this as if to say, "Václav had his ceremony at an early age, and Boleslav is as worthy."

Great things were expected of me.

I was given a sword.

The pagans of the town came to the sacred glade that morning to witness the presentation. Many townspeople still held to Christianity, though not openly. Most Christians, poor ones, did not attend any pagan ceremonies.

Mother had a simple wooden throne and canopy brought to the forest clearing, and as she walked into the field, music played from a zither, fanfrnochs and davul drums. Veshtak and his men were there in a group, beside my mother. She started wearing a fine cloak in public, trimmed in white ermine fur. She wore a circlet of silver on her head, emulating princesses and queens in the Frankish Empire. When she sat on the throne, two men blew blasts from great war horns.

Dušan stepped forward to face the throne and the crowd, and motioned I should stand before him.

They dressed me in a battle tunic of my size, and I wore a chain metal hauberk and steel helmet. Around my waist was a new leather belt inscribed with runes of power, studded with polished iron rivets.

That outfit was heavy in the warming sun of late spring.

Dušan placed his hands on my shoulders and said in a loud voice, "This is the son of Vratislav, Prince of Bohemia, and of Dragomira!" Many in the audience remembered their brave ruler, and his childless brother who preceded him on the ducal throne.

"May he be blessed by Svantovít and Veles, and wield this sword in defense of his land, and do justice to our enemies!" The crowd, led by Tunna, cried, "Slava! Glory!"

Dušan turned to his assistant Kamil, who handed the sword to the priest. Dušan buckled the sword to my belt and stood back.

I grasped the handle and drew the blade from its scabbard. I held it high. It flashed in sunlight, and the crowd cheered.

This was a full-sized sword, heavy, not like the smaller wooden swords or the dirk I had used in training. It was a wonder of the bladesmith's art, with a strong, gleaming blade, broad and as long as my leg, with a fuller as wide as my thumbprint running nearly its entire length. The metal was Dušan's good steel, and the hand guard curved like a crescent moon, decorated with engravings of sacred oak leaves. Its balance was good. I would grow into it.

I thought then of what name I should give it.

"Behold grandson of Bořivoj, Prince of Bohemia, and of Ludmila." I heard a murmur from the audience at the name of my honored, murdered grandmother. Some in the audience fondly held those rulers in their hearts, those two who did their best for their people, regardless of their religion. They brought the Czechs closer to the more advanced cultures of Europe. And they wisely permitted those who wished, to keep the faith of the old gods as the nation grew closer to the community of Christendom.

Dušan said, "We call mighty Svantovít to bless this prince and let him mature in his strength to defend our land, and to show proper fealty to his older brother Václav when he comes to rule!" Several in the crowd cheered quietly. Some did not.

At that statement Veshtak leaned and spoke softly to Mother, who nodded and signaled the service was over.

The horns were again winded, and their sound echoed to the forest.

Mother stood, instruments played, the rhythm of drums and fanfrnochs throbbed amid the tune of the zither. Veshtak walked nearly abreast of her, and his knights and pages followed.

Before leaving, Dušan looked down at me with his clear blue eye. He was not smiling now, but slowly nodded his head as if to confirm in my heart the words he had just spoken: "… fealty to our people and his older brother…" Years later, after my sins, even today, I devote my life to honor that prayer. Too late! Pray for me, Kristián!

The priest and Kamil turned and walked away in the morning sunlight, and the crowd dispersed.

Tira and Tuza came to me and we walked from the field.

Tuza said, "Now you can use a real weapon when we go into the wood. You have a real sword!"

I told them I'd considered calling it "Slavný," meaning "Glorious."

Tuza said, "'Tvůrce Králů! That is the name for your blade! 'Kingmaker!'" I liked the sound of it. Only later did I realize what the name would portend.

***

Mother sent Saskia to my chamber the night of receiving the blade from Dušan.

She had continued as a wet nurse to leading families of Prague, and her milk still flowed well. The poor slave's life was little better than a dairy cow, passed from infant to infant for the convenience of their mothers.

Saskia was solemn, quiet. She stepped into the room and dropped the shawl that was covering her chest. "Boleslav. Your mother…" I saw new welts on her shoulders and neck, evidence of Mother's displeasure, perhaps at Saskia's reticence of her task to me.

She was not an ugly woman. She still had beauty, though nearly thirty years old. As I looked at her body, I felt a tightness of my throat. I could hear my heartbeat in my eardrums, and felt blood rushing through me. I had a confusion of emotions for this bare-breasted woman, still attractive to men—to me.

I said, "Saskia. I feel different tonight. I am not at ease."

I knew she was unhappy with her position, a loveless, childless slave, abused by her owner, forced to waste the life the gods had given her in an unjust effort of my mother to control me, her own flesh son.

I cleared my throat and turned my eyes away from her. "Cover yourself," I said.

She said, "Your mother…"

I again told her to cover herself. Then I handed her my purse. It held three silver pennies and some coppers I had acquired from travelers through our city, as well as two folded squares of cloth of value. She pulled her clothes on, though she looked frightened. I told her to flee the city, away from the power of Mother and those in her influence. She should go to the Jewish quarter and seek a man there named Jakob, and give him the cloths in the pouch. I said, "Tell him I want you to have safe passage to the west, to the kingdom of the Franks. Jakob will treat you well."

She slowly took the purse from my hand and looked about her. This night she ceased being a slave. This night, the night they gave me my sword "Kingmaker," my mother lost power over Saskia.

In sending my nurse away I took a bit of power onto myself, which I had not done before. It was years until I took genuine power unto myself—too much at first—until I learned to give up some of it, perhaps too late for my soul's salvation.

But everyone must learn to do that in his way, I suppose, and in his own time.

She smiled at me and hugged me goodbye.

I felt her arms about me, her warmth. I was conscious of the shape of her body against my chest. In my confusion I gently pushed her away and said, "Go in secret. Go now, kind Saskia."

She put the purse in a pocket of her cloak and left for the Jewish quarter, to my family friend from the days of my grandfather, the old duke.

The coins in the pouch were struck in the Frankish kingdom and had a Frankish king's face on them. We had no coins of our own manufacture then. I am perhaps sinful in my pride of being our first ruler to have had coins minted, celebrating my marriage to your mother. But in those times we had no coins. We conducted our trade in barter, of honey, furs, grain, iron nails, tools, knives, and in squares of cloth representing an obligation.

Two such cloths were in the pouch I sent with Saskia.

Our family did a favor for Jakob the Trader, granting him rights to buy and sell goods and slaves in our town and on our protected trade routes. We granted him the right to build homes for his family and relations in Prague.

Jews are among the most successful traders. When they were driven from their homes in the Holy Lands, they settled in many regions. They kept their peculiar language and writing, so wherever Jews traveled, they could speak with others of their race. They took wives from families of their distant cousins there.

The Jews of Prague have lived here for centuries. Grandmother's friend Jakob has regular communication with others of his tribe in distant places. It was to his care I sent Saskia, paid for with an obligation he owed my grandmother and her dead husband the old duke, represented by those cloths.

The coins were for Saskia.

Coins make more sense for travel, and maybe for everything. Roman coins are still in use when they can be found. Coinage from London in Britain, or from Brussels, Venice, Constantinople all come through our city. And if you must, you can use the metals of coins for their own value, such as to craft into silver jewelry. Or to hammer into a plate or pot, if you have enough copper pennies. Scrap bits of copper, silver and gold by weight have value, but a coin of standard value is much easier to trade.

So my nursemaid, with safe passage to the land of the Franks, had enough money to live until she could find herself a situation.

I never again saw the woman named Saskia.

＊

Our city sits on an important and ancient road. Following ancient routes, traders and merchants travel west to Plzeň, Leipzig and Bruges, or north to Breslau, and to the sea at Gdansk where there is amber. The road travels south to Linz, Innsbruck, all the way to Venice and Rome where there are mighty buildings of marble stone, and to the East. One could set foot on the road to Libická, Brno, Belgrade, to Constantinople, and even farther, to the very end of the world where strange people live, with strange ways and strange gods.

Goods flow along that road, and ideas. From Prague we trade good iron, ornaments and precious furs of mink and ermine, hides of leather, silver jewelry and honey, linen cloth and wools. In exchange we receive wines, items of transparent glass, and amber. From the east come seeds of new plants, and cloth we're told is made of spider webs, new spices, and inventions and recipes. Dušan often hosted and offered shelter to travelers, and learned new things from them. Some travelers were strange to me, with lidless squinting eyes and colorful shiny robes.

People at the ends of the roads have different ideas of religion. Some believe men—and even women—are born into the world bearing the soul of someone who has lived and died before. Some believe the sun is itself God. Many believe in a prophet who tells them living a virtuous life will result in you becoming one with heaven.

There are many such ideas and beliefs I cannot comprehend or tell properly. Never mind that! We have our great prophets written of in the Holy Scriptures!

But I can say it is obvious that men need to believe in something. And not all have heard the words of Jesus, or want to listen to the ideas of men unlike themselves.

Every man wants a connection with God, or with gods, or with something. We had pagan gods and our best understanding of them before the Holy Brothers brought the words of Jesus to the people.

Some of His words are not much different from what Dušan told us. Perhaps one day, all men will share the same style of living and worshipping.

Perhaps not.

So, these ideas, goods, habits, tools, inventions, foods and beliefs travel the world over pathways as old as mankind. Kristián, you will travel a bit of that road when you go to Regensburg.

Trains of pack horses, donkeys and other animals travel these roads with armed men to protect the traders from bandits. Kings guard many roads because of the good their courts receive from safe travel routes, but many segments of roads are deserted of civilization, and there are pirates in remote places.

And do you know, Kristián, there are pirates among us, here where we live?

***

I grew older in the company of Tuza and his younger, gentler brother Tira, as they matured into manhood, still tending me, directing my thoughts and attitudes.

They continued to assure me I was as a prince privileged, and could behave as a ruler to strangers we met. They were now strong young men, armed with sword, dirk and axe, and would defend any wish I had.

Tunna had given his sons new horses, and they were eager to test them on trails through the forest. So, we three went to the stables and rode into the dark woods seeking adventure.

Tunna and Gomon grew in wealth using their friendship with Mother. They were each prideful and Mother, seeing their increasing strength, distanced herself from them, and encouraged competition between them. The two grew to hate each other, each blaming the other for crimes both of them had committed, and each continuing to take goods and stock from the homesteads of peasants. They grew their wealth through theft and banditry.

Gomon and Tunna finally made public declarations against each other, called each other scoundrel and thief, and both raided each other's estates.

Sheep were driven off, fields trampled, cows killed. Finally, their pride and rivalry drove them to murder.

One moonlit night, Gomon's men were away on a hunt, leaving just women and children at his property. Tunna, along with his sons Tuza and Tira, crept onto his lands to steal horses. Unknown to Tunna, Gomon had stayed behind, suspecting Tunna's thievery if he believed Gomon was absent from his home.

Dogs called the alarm, and the giant Gomon flew from his home bearing a large mace. He leapt and struck Tunna with a single blow to the chest, and knocked his old friend and conspirator senseless. He turned to the brothers Tuza and Tira and said, "Take him away. When he awakes, if he does, tell him I banish him and all his family from these lands, and all of Bohemia. This hammer can deal many blows." And Gomon lifted his mace and shattered a stone on the ground.

Now Gomon had no legal right to do any banishing. It takes a lord or law to do that. But the image of this giant and his great weapon in the moonlight, and their gasping father stricken at their feet made the sons of Tunna do as they were ordered. They carried their father away, and when he had regained his mind, if not his whole body, Tunna was afraid. He asked his two sons to take him back to the lands of his birth, where he soon died.

Tuza and Tira returned to Prague and found me. Mother seemed pleased at the way things happened and welcomed them back to her court. They were in her debt now, and stayed close to me, knowing the power of the ducal seat would protect them from Gomon and his men.

Mother continued to spin her plans and consolidate her power.

***

I turned thirteen, then fourteen, nearing maturity and taking the shape of a man. I grew hair where adults have hair, and to notice girls I passed in town. One night of celebration of spring I danced the circle dance, and the girl holding my hand drew me away and into the woods. In my youthful ignorance, I fumbled with her body and my own until she laughed at my callow inexperience. She left me embarrassed, to find herself a more practiced mate for an evening's joy.

***

I continued my weapons practice, and on my fifteenth birthday, Hněvsa and Tira took me to the house where Tira and Tuza stayed, and they fed me mead and round cookies with fruit jam in the middle.

Then Tuza came through the door and brought with him a girl slave he had bought at the town market. They knew I had not yet been with a woman.

She was probably sixteen years old. She spoke with an accent from the east, similar to that of Kamil, Dušan's apprentice.

Many slaves passed through our town, a stop on their ways to far roads to the rest of their lives.

The slave was dressed in a simple brown shift, fairly clean. Her mood was not happy, but resigned. Her story was probably much like those of other slaves.

Raids captured most slaves, with men, babies and old people killed, boys taken to the house of castration or sold as laborers, and girls and young women sold into female bondage.

My friends, with some little instruction, left her with me.

I had seen breeding of horses, dogs and other animals, so I understood the physical mechanics. She had doubtless been used by several men in days after her capture and knew resistance would not help her. Her best course at this point was to prove her value by performing well and hope for the hour's partner to be kind. She went to the bed and sat upon it.

Despite my fifteen years of maturity, I was hesitant. My throat tightened, as it had when I last saw Saskia unrobed. As the young woman lifted her shift over her head, I could not take my eyes from her body.

Now, you must understand, Kristián, I was totally new to physical relations, other than fondling and pinching girls after a circle dance around fires that summer, and I had not met your mother yet.

The way Tuza and Tira talked of this subject made it seem I should be able to dominate and proudly perform on women, and have them screaming in giddy pleasure.

But I thought of Saskia, my nurse, and the sadness of her life, denied even the simple pleasure of seeing her child play and grow into adulthood.

So, my actions that night with the slave girl were tempered with memories of my wetnurse. But the girl was, if not eager, at least compliant, and she obliged my clumsy advances. What other choice was there for her?

The activity quickly became an end in itself. My thoughts of other things were swept up in sensations of the moment. My body was quickly satisfied, and with a shock of physical thrill, sated. After a few moments and a shared pastry, I repeated my pleasure in her.

I fell asleep, and when I awoke, the girl was gone, taken by Tuza and Tira for their use, and then back to the slave market. When I asked about her, Tuza said not to worry about her, and told me I was too tenderhearted to really enjoy life.

But he said I could change.

CHAPTER 5
Srpen—The Time of Harvest

My older brother Václav finally reached the age when he could rule. As such, he should take control of the Ducal lands and powers. We celebrated this with a ceremony denoting becoming a ruler.

It also would mean the end of Mother's regency.

In August, after the feast of midsummer we call "Koupel," my brother Václav returned from Budeč with a small retinue. He had inherited Grandmother Ludmila's old servant Mstena, who traveled with him, as did his page Podiven. The page was now a free young Christian man—tall, strong, fiercely loyal to Václav.

Six armed men and three servants accompanied them, and so did a Christian priest—a German Frank named Erhard. Two of the armed men were Danes. They had become Christians and had dedicated their lives to the service of their new religion, using the tools at their hands to help its growth.

When the party arrived in Prague, Václav came boldly to the house of our dead father, and his pages forced open the chapel last used by Ludmila. They prayed and lit candles to her memory, those three who had known Ludmila—Mstena, Podiven, and Václav. They spent some time kneeling in prayer as their armed men guarded them from disturbance, even when Veshtak's men Tuza and Tira sought to enter.

Of the three kneeling in prayer all were solid men, but Podiven was a striking figure. He was Václav's best friend and defender. He owed his freedom and faith to Ludmila and to her memory, now embodied in Václav.

Václav's return was expected, yet it was a challenge to Mother and her followers. It was heartening to people who had loved Grandmother

Ludmila. Many still practiced Christian customs, mostly in secret, to avoid the attention of my mother Dragomira, and of Veshtak and his men.

Václav was mature now. He was a strong young man of eighteen, ready and resolved to assume his country's throne.

***

He sent word to all hamlets, crofts, and Czech villages that he would take his throne on a sunny day that winter, and he invited all to attend, especially nobles and their knights.

Václav's Christian priest, Erhard, had a quiet meeting with the pagan priest Dušan and told him of Václav's plans for the ceremony. He also shared with him it was to be a Christian ceremony, and out of respect for Václav's religious faith, Dušan said he would meet with Václav another time in private. They had much to discuss. Dušan spread the word to his followers to be present at the ceremony to support the new duke, and to bring their weapons, many he had provided.

Mother would be there, and she would bring nobles who supported her. Veshtak would bring his armed men, pagans who followed his ways.

Nobles came to Prague in the days before the coronation ceremony. They erected tents around the city, and there were meetings and reunions, fires to keep them warm where they shared stories and sporting games.

Some visited the pagan priest Dušan and his iron works, where his men showed them knives and swords and axes being made. Some men bought weapons, and some placed orders.

Others sought out Veshtak, and they spoke of what tomorrow would bring.

Many went to Prince Václav's house to meet with him. They were relieved he was back. Christianity would find welcome in Prague again.

Václav ended the evening at Ludmila's chapel in prayer with his pages and the priest, and they prayed for the morrow's success, with God's grace. He asked his priest Erhard to read aloud from the Holy Scripture that Methodius and Cyril had written in our language, but since he read and spoke only German and Latin, Václav read from the book. Some passages from Psalms could have been written for the occasion:

"Help, LORD, for no one is faithful anymore;
    those who are loyal have vanished from our people.
Everyone lies to their neighbor;
    they flatter with their lips but harbor double hearts.
May the Lord silence all flattering lips
    and every boastful tongue—
You, Lord, will keep the needy safe
    and will protect us forever from the wicked,
Who freely strut about when what is vile
    is honored by the human race.
Through you we push back our enemies;
    through your name we trample our foes.
You give us victory over our enemies;
    you put our adversaries to shame.
Therefore, you kings, be wise;
    be warned, you rulers of the earth.
Serve the Lord with fear
    and celebrate his rule with trembling."

People expected Mother to raise a challenge to Václav's ascension to power despite his universally acknowledged right to do so. These Christians were preparing themselves for a contest, and the priest quoted scripture:

"The Lord is my rock and my fortress
  and my deliverer;
My God, my strength,
  in whom I will trust;
My shield and the horn of my salvation,
  my stronghold.
I will call upon the Lord with praises,
  and I shall be saved from my enemies."

***

The next morning was cool and sunny in the plaza outside the palace.

Nobles lined the great yard crowding the scene, all in their best fur robes, each with an attendant.

Some wore crosses on chains around their necks, a public display of Christianity not seen in years. Everyone had heard of Václav's strong fealty to the Christian faith and of his mild ways. Some expected he would not take the throne, but become a monk and leave the country.

All attending, both pagan and Christian, were armed, some with long daggers, some with swords, some with small maces on their belts. Many had armor under their robes.

Veshtak and his men stood at one end of the rise by the dais where Dragomira's wooden throne was set, flanked by Tuza and Tira, sons of dead Tunna. They gave stern looks at gray-haired Gomon, Tunna's old killer. His men surrounded him, and he stood apart from the rest of Dragomira's followers.

Mother again dressed herself in a "royal robe," as she called it, and again wore the circlet of silver.

A blast from a war horn signaled her entrance, and she proudly stepped into the plaza in her cream-white ermine. I walked beside her in awe that all these people, displaying their wealth, would come to show obeisance to my brother. And many, perhaps, to Mother.

When she was seated, two musicians entered the plaza hammering on dulcimers suspended in front of them by straps about their waists and neck. The music they played sounded like a gentle cloud of joy as they slowly paced into the plaza and up to the stone seat where dukes were crowned. They stood on either side of the empty throne, continuing their music, and the priest Erhard, who had come with Václav from Budeč, entered carrying a smoking censer. As he slowly moved up the broad aisle of the plaza, the smoke's fragrance infused the crowd with a false sense of calm.

Podiven entered next, holding high the great sword of Václav, "Faith's Defender," as he paced to his place to the right of the throne.

Next came Václav.

His head was newly shaved around the sides, with a leather skullcap atop his wheat-colored hair. He wore a simple white tunic over a suit of fine mail, though whether this was to display a kingly radiance of wealth or to afford actual protection from an attack I never learned. It's not a bad policy, though. I maintain it for myself.

His air was cool and determined. He saw this as the challenge of his life, to take up the power of the traditional ducal throne from his mother, left him by his killed father.

Two Christian Danes followed him armed with great swords, and the rest of his retinue entered, including Mstena.

As he entered the plaza, Mstena turned and looked at Mother and at Veshtak, and his men. In the cool sunlight I saw Gomon recognize him, and Mstena recognized one of the killers of his mistress Ludmila. Each held the other in a steady gaze.

Václav looked at Gomon and the men surrounding Mother, then at Mstena, who bent his head to my brother's and whispered into his ear.

Václav's face became a mask of dismay, and then hardened into a stern resolve. He stood. His face was stone.

After a pause he knelt before the throne and was blessed by the Catholic priest. On this greatest day of his life he recognized the treachery of his mother against Ludmila, his adored and saintly grandmother.

I saw eyes flicker about in the crowd. All waited, with different members looking for a sign from Gomon, or from Podiven, or Veshtak. There was no overt sign, though nervous hands strayed to hilts of swords. The forces supporting Václav and those for Mother seemed evenly matched.

Time balanced on a knife's edge. A determined move by either faction would meet equal resistance by the other.

It was my brother who took initiative and gained the day.

He rose from his kneeling place and stepped up to the throne.

As he lowered himself upon the ancient throne of Bohemian dukes from time immemorial, he raised his right hand, palm open. A great blaring of horns from outside the plaza stunned the crowd. This was not a formal fanfare such as musicians played at the courts of Frankish kings. This was a deep and loud raw blast, war horns letting loose a sound of power. The shocking and sustained roar played for ten beats of my heart, and I felt a rush of blood to my face.

Everyone was excited, alerted by the noise.

At another wave from the duke's hand, the horns stopped, and the new duke stood in broad sunlight, tall, a man of strength and power.

"I know of intrigues now riling my people." Václav's eyes were on our mother, Dragomira.

All looked at Mother. I stood beside her and was washed in her mortification.

Duke Václav continued to the crowd, "You are my faithful people, yet many are not in Christ!"

Veshtak glanced about him nervously.

"When I was sent by my parents to my studies, I learned a lesson from Paul, the Apostle of Jesus. Paul said, 'When I was a child, I spoke as a child. When I became a man, I put away childish things.'"

The new duke continued, "I have examined my heart. I discovered my wretchedness, desiring to take up my father's title and power, my own lusting for fame and riches. Eldest of birth among brothers, the title is mine, yet I was still a child."

His eyes swept over the crowd. "Today I put away my childhood, and take up my father's birthright!

"By the Lord's Command and strengthened by the mercy of the Most High, I will resist and give no heed to untruths of malicious people." His gaze gripped the assembly, and he paused. A change came over him. A calm questioning replaced the warning of his wrath.

"Why did you evil-doers, liars and iniquitous people hinder me from studying the Divine Laws of Jesus Christ? What right have you in denying me or anyone the right to serve God? I was under your control, but today I throw it off! I will serve God and follow his laws with my whole heart!

"Let the love of peace rise in my domain. Let no affair before any court be judged wrongly and contrary to fact!" He paused again, and called loudly, "All intrigues end this day!" His supporters cheered wildly, and many others joined in. His voice swelled.

"Let conspiracies and gatherings of evil among you cease! Do not commit murder any more. If fear of the god of Abraham does not keep you from transgressing His law, know my own wrath will blaze against such evildoers, and we will strike off the heads of the guilty!" My brother, gentle Václav, did not speak in this way often.

He raised his hand again and the war horns blared to mark an end to the ceremony. No one was in doubt that we now had a duke.

With a stern warning glare, he ordered Mother banished from our land. She and her household refuged far away, to the east with the Croats.

Veshtak vanished from our city, and Tuza and Tira moved to the village where in years to come I built my castle stronghold.

In the weeks following his coronation my brother became a very active duke, beloved by most, but not everyone.

It is not always clear when things are going well.

***

Tuza and Tira had stayed close to Mother. Before she exiled to the east, with her quiet approval, they sought vengeance on Gomon, killer of their father. Mother had long disliked Gomon because of his independence from her, and the brothers knew they should act now.

Blood feuds have been a part of life from ancient days, and I expect they always will. I shudder to think God may carry one on me.

The sons of Tunna were in their eighteenth and twenty-first years. Gomon was older, more than 45 years of age, and he was gray and stiff in his knees. But he was still a formidable man and could wield his heavy mace.

Three nights after Václav's ceremony, some confederates of Tuza and Tira started a fire in the forest at the edge of Gomon's properties, by the pasture where he kept his cattle.

An alarm was shouted and Gomon's men ran to save the cows from the fire, and maybe from cattle thieves. Gomon watched in his nightclothes from atop the steps by his doorway.

When his men were all across the fields, Tira nocked an arrow to his bowstring and sent it into the belly of Gomon. This surprised the big man, and as he drew it from his stomach, another flew into his chest. He sat down and watched as Tuza leapt upon him with his sword.

When he swung the sword, the big man blocked it with his arm. Despite wounds in his torso and his broken arm, Gomon was still a dangerous opponent. He stood and charged at Tuza, using the weight of his body as a weapon.

Tuza was young and spry. He leapt aside and as the big man's inertia swept past him, he laid a stroke across the side of his attacker, which laid open his body and spilled him onto the ground.

Tuza neared the gasping giant and whispered, "So do the sons of Tunna take their vengeance."

Another stroke ensured Gomon could never tell the tale of his killers.

His woman exited the hut and screamed. Tuza's sword made quick work of her and her two young sons. Then Tira and Tuza left the homestead, and no one ever learned who had murdered Gomon until Tira told me years later.

I expect many knew just who it was, though.

Beware of blood feuds, my son. They often have no end!

Duke Václav was as good or better than his words.

He traveled all over the lands of his control, often accompanied by his servant Podiven. He walked humbly in bare feet, wearing a simple hood over a hair shirt in penance for sins he felt within himself. And to his eyes, he did commit a few, though many commit worse without regrets.

Václav recognized he had impure thoughts. Sometimes he was burdened by rule and by his inability to cleanse all the land of sin. He would despair and sometimes drink mead or wine to where he did not clearly follow Christian law. He would act impulsively and even lasciviously to women, or treat people unkindly and curse those around him. The next morning he would be regretful, and spent hours in prayer for forgiveness, seeking to make amends for his transgressions.

It may be his humanity, his repentance for common human faults that all of us have, which made him so beloved by the people.

After such sinful behavior he ate only greens for days in penance, and also as a cleansing purge for his body. When he realized he had deviated from the righteous path, he corrected his steps. Then he would rise and do good works.

Several times he talked with me, and he would open his heart. I was his brother, and though we had not grown up together since I was very young, I was his closest living relative, except for our sisters who had already been married to distant lands. Dragomira had made a home with the Croats.

Václav was open and honest with me, and shared feelings about being more suited to holy work than being a duke. But he recognized he had a duty and could benefit his people as their leader, and so he did.

His life tallied a lengthening list of good deeds for people wherever he went, often without revealing his identity. He and his humble retinue dressed in plain clothes, Václav usually barefoot, and his party was often unrecognized. They helped farmers pick grapes, plant and harvest wheat and millet, cut wood and gather honey.

Wherever he went, he was an example of goodness, mercy, charity, so like Grandmother Ludmila. He spread the Word of the Gospel and Christianized many in our dukedom by his example.

When he became overwhelmed with his tasks and became intemperate in action or words, he worked all the more intensely in days that followed.

Through his good works and generosity many of his subjects, especially around the towns, converted to the Faith. The duke and his priests oversaw pulling down of pagan idols. They converted sites sacred to the pagan gods Svantovít and Veles into shrines to the holy Christian Svatý Vít, known by the Romans as Saint Vitus, or to Svatý Michael, or the Blessed Virgin Svatá Mary. Many holy sites in Slavic lands were dedicated to Svatý Vít because his name was so similar to the pagan god Svantovít, and made it easier for people to accept him as an important saint. It also helped that he is patron saint of dance, so the kolo circle dance of the pagans could be incorporated—or at least accepted into some Christian ceremonies, though without overt sexual revelry at its climax.

There was often reluctance to supplanting old gods with the new scheme of saints surrounding worship of Jesus. Yet, by his works of charity, Václav personified such human goodness to his subjects that he was nearly universally loved.

Václav secretly made gifts of grain or wine or firewood to unsuspecting poor peasants. He regularly visited the slave market, bought and fed slaves, converted and freed them. Many of his converts became very loyal to him. Some Christian men he freed went to work at the ironworks, still managed by the pagan priest Dušan.

Wherever he went, Václav had Podiven and his servants carry with them a portable grinding mill, a quern. He took wheat he helped harvest and milled it into flour, which he formed and baked into biscuits for mass, and served them with his priest as the Holy Eucharist.

There are many tales of his personal goodness. One popular story many people tell is this one:

On the night after the mass for Christ's birth as Václav finished his evening meal, he opened a window in his hall looked out onto the snowy field to the forest beyond his palace fence. Against the white ground, he saw a peasant picking up branches fallen from trees because of a heavy snow. The man piled them on a sledge and dragged it behind him to the next deadfalls.

Václav had compassion on his subject. He called Podiven to take some meat and bread from the table and a skin of wine, and go with him to where the peasant was working. On the way out, Václav gave an order that a great load of firewood borne by workers follow him that very night.

The air was cold, and the men were robed against it, though Václav was barefoot again. Podiven followed Václav in deep snow. The bright moon lit the sky in a glow, and light seemed to come from the white earth like an inverted day. The peasant had set off for home and passed into woods.

Václav asked if he knew the man and Podiven replied he did, though he lived two thousand paces away by a fountain sacred to the old religion. Podiven said it was too dark and too late, and suggested they should return to the warmth of the castle hearth.

My brother said, "Let us find this peasant. I feel we can bring Christian charity to him this night."

Podiven replied to him, "My feet, Lord, are so cold. And yours have no shoes!"

Václav smiled. "I am fine and have warmth for both of us. Walk in my footsteps and yours will be warmed."

Václav's feet were cracked and bleeding, which was not unusual for my brother. His faith was stronger than his pain and he gave this no mind, though his prints showed a trace of his blood. Podiven marched along, more concerned for his master than for his own comfort.

They followed the trail of the peasant's sled, and within dark woods the trees wailed in the windy sky above them. Podiven looked at the treetops and saw moonlight glancing off their ice-covered needles and branches, reflected as if there were slivers of light among twigs and greenery.

Ahead of them, they saw the shadowy shape of the peasant dragging his firewood. And there were lights in the forest. Someone, the peasant's wife, I suppose, had left a few wax candles within small skin lanterns along the trail as guiding lights for the man and his sled of winter fuel.

He turned off the trail to his small homestead, a hut near a brook, and started carrying his wood inside.

"Hail, citizen!" cried Václav.

The peasant spun to see two dark figures approaching his home, and reached for a stone knife tucked in his belt.

"Fear not, subject!" said the duke.

The peasant recognized Václav and fell to his knees in the snow.

My brother told him to "Rise, and be of good cheer! We bring gifts!"

The humble man opened his door and offered shelter from the cold to the duke.

Václav and Podiven stepped down and ducked to enter the tiny hut. The amazed peasant's wife bowed. The peasant and his pregnant wife had a girl toddler.

These home shelters are just one room, with a curtained alcove where mats laid on the floor and another where baskets store apples and turnips, millet and wheat. A crude loom was in a corner near the doorway, with wool threads on it. A clay hearth was at the eastern side of the room, which had a vent in the roof for smoke. By the fire stood a small stone figure of a bearded man bent with age. He represented the ancient ancestral spirit of the family.

The humble home had bits of evergreen around, a pagan symbol of Morana, the spirit of life in the deadness of winter. Václav told Podiven to share the food and wine with them.

Václav prayed in the name of Christ over the food and for the family.

Then the duke took a holy biscuit symbolizing the Eucharist and tied it to an evergreen branch, thus consecrating that pagan tree as a Christian symbol.

As he did this, bearers of firewood arrived for the poor family. Václav gave the master of the house a folded cloth of value and demanded a promise they would pray at the nearest church on the next sabbath.

Václav and Podiven left with Christian blessings on the family, and strode home with the slaves who had brought wood. He committed himself to return to the nearby pagan spring and consecrate it to a Christian saint.

Václav hummed an ancient hymn he heard at a ceremony of Dušan. It was an old Czech tune, and he fitted it with Christian lyrics. It became a Christian song of the grace of Jesus.

This is one of many tales of the duke's good works.

***

During my brother's time as ruler, our land was challenged and beset by invasions and wars from the Franks, and by pagan and half-Christianized tribes from the south and east.

Václav saw the need to defend our lands and began a program of organizing the warriors of Bohemia. He spent funds for standardized weaponry, armor, and for training, so he could rely on a common strength of different elements of his army. This was a significant improvement over the prior system of each village's fighters arming themselves as they could and raiding in their own ways.

In one period of uprising, he gathered his forces and led them to meet the rebels. On the way to the field of battle he saw a young girl holding a withe from a willow tree, waving and pointing at troops as they crossed a bridge. One by one she pointed her stick at them, and Václav wept because he knew many of his countrymen would die on the field, perhaps as many as the little child would point to. He imagined he could count each doomed man as he passed him, and he wanted to avoid battles if he could. But too often he could not.

He believed warfare was sometimes necessary, but it was not good Christian practice.

Many pagan leaders saw Václav's accession to the ducal throne as a chance to break away from the rule of Prague. The new duke was not yet in his full strength, and all knew his nature was peaceful because of his faith.

Late one season when the harvest was being brought in from the fields, a chieftain named Radslav of Kourim sought to break his tribe away, to rule his district without paying tribute to the duke. He began attacks to loot villages beyond the borders of his lands.

Václav knew he must meet this challenge to ducal power.

He called his forces together and marched them to the east. An advance party of Václav's men met some forces of Kourim, and after a brief and sharp fight, each side retreated and made camp. The duke posted skirmishers and sentinels as his men made camp and prepared for the next day's battle.

Václav learned of the day's skirmish and counted his dead and wounded. He was mindful of lives in his care, and again sought to avoid the killing of men, both his forces and those of his rebellious subjects. He took council with his priest Erhard and then sent his servant Podiven on a secret mission to achieve his goals in a way that avoided further loss of life.

Podiven left camp on foot and went into the forest after sunset. He hid his sword in some bushes and circled to the rear of the enemy's camp. While well outside their lines, he fit a white cover over the top of his head and unfurled a large white flag on a short pole. Then he blew a blast from a horn, and stood in the middle of the field behind their camp unarmed, slowly waving the flag, to await Radslav's sentries to take him prisoner.

Radslav's men approached him cautiously, fearing a ruse of some sort.

Podiven told the men he bore an important message for their chief from the duke, and was led to the chief's orderly. Radslav was notified, and they brought Podiven into his tent under guard. The leader was with his captains planning the next day's battle.

A Christian and a pagan priest were both in the tent. The pagan, short, wizened and missing an eye, was throwing divining bones near the fire. The Christian was speaking to Radslav.

When Podiven came near the fire, he drew from his pocket six small sticks and laid them before the chief. He said the words Václav had told him:

"Honored and valiant Chieftain, my lord Václav, Duke of the Czechs, has bidden me share this ancient truth with you.

"There are forces from the north, east, and south that wish to break our strength and steal our grain, our goods, to kill and enslave our people. They will steal boys and girls, and kill infants at their mothers' breasts, leaving them to wail in their pain, and to suckle puppies instead of their children.

"As individual tribes, we cannot stand against them."

Podiven picked up a stone from the fire ring and drove it against one stick, and broke it. He looked up at Radslav. Then he gathered the remaining five sticks and tied them tightly together with a bit of twine from his pocket. He lifted the stone again and struck the bundle, which did not break.

"See—look how together we can stand against invaders and protect our homes and families."

Podiven then told the chief and his captains the duke sent terms they could find agreeable, and he would relate these to them if they could speak privately, without priests hearing his words.

Despite their protests Radslav sent away the priests and all but one of his captains to hear his message.

In early morning darkness, Podiven returned to the camp of the duke's forces. As the army was awakening and preparing for battle Podiven spoke with the duke.

Day was breaking with few clouds in a clear blue sky. The two armies went to the field and organized themselves into battle array with spearmen, archers, and cavalry. The Czech infantry stood at a relaxed attention. Each man had a round wooden shield covered with hardened leather, and held a short spear which could stab or could be thrown like a javelin. All wore iron-studded leather jerkins and helmets bound with iron, and all carried a long dirk. The horsemen were similarly armed, though they also carried swords, and each had a war hammer.

The opposing forces of Radslav, though more numerous than the duke's, were equipped as each man or his lord saw fit and could afford. They appeared more as a large raiding party than a disciplined force.

Václav sent his page Podiven to the center of the field, again dressed in a white over-tunic and bearing a white flag. A man from Kourim walked to meet him, also carrying a white banner. As the man came close to Václav's page, Podiven turned to look at the display of Václav's army, standing in disciplined lines with their shields held before them and their spears in their right hands. He then turned his eyes on the Kourim host, and the emissary from Radslav did the same. The disparity in equipment and readiness was stark. The two pages faced each other again. Podiven spoke the words Václav had told him.

Following ancient tradition, each army agreed they would abide by decision of a battle of champions, Václav in single combat against Radslav. Had those two armies met and fought that day, there would be death and sorrow on both sides, but the victorious outcome for Václav's Czechs, well-armed and trained, was not in doubt.

Václav, though strong, armored in iron helmet and trained in swordcraft, was not as robust nor tall as the Kourim chief. If these two fought, the odds would favor Radslav.

Václav bided his time until the sun broke away from clouds, and then he rode slowly from the north to meet in bright sunshine with the rebel chieftain. Radslav rode from his army onto the flat field. Each man wore shiny armor polished for display in battle.

When they were within twenty paces of one another, as sunlight fell upon Duke Václav, his helmet sparkled. Rivets on his helmet and the crucifix metal brow flashed. The rebel chief stopped his horse, dismounted and fell to his knees, dropped his sword and shouted, "Oh Lord Jesus, I see Your Sign of the Cross on the brow of Duke Václav! I see him surrounded by a host of angels! I submit myself to your will!" Václav walked to the kneeling chief and knelt himself, and put his hand on the shoulder of Radslav. The men both prayed for a few moments as the restless men of Kourim and the rigid troops of Prague gazed at the two leaders.

The challenge and apprehension of conflict passed from the field with the morning breeze.

Both leaders stood and called their priests to the center of the field. Podiven carried a satchel and accompanied Václav's priest, Erhard.

When they met, the two Christian priests turned to Radslav's pagan priest and said, "Go from this place! The Lord Jesus Christ rules here!"

The one-eyed pagan rapidly fled the field.

The two Christian priests together consecrated the meeting of the leaders. As Václav and Radslav again knelt, the priests shared in prayer. From Podiven's satchel they ate bread ground and baked by Václav, and drank wine from Grandmother Ludmila's vineyard. On that field where there would have been a human sacrifice of a thousand men, the two leaders shared holy Christian Communion.

Václav said, "A vision from God has given me wisdom to see a way to peace. Your people will leave the villages of our land and return to their own. They will keep their mounts, their farms, their arms. We will renew alliances among us and surrounding lands for mutual protection. You, Radslav, will rule your lands as long as you live, and we, Duke of Bohemia, will be your tribute lord.

"And your people will share with mine the love of Christ."

So, the territory was brought more firmly under the duke's control, and was further Christianized. Resentment remained among men who had wished to battle and sack the towns, now rich with grain from the harvest.

And some still wished to keep pagan ways.

***

For the celebration of my seventeenth birthday, Tira, Tuza and Hněvsa took me to a house in a nearby village where a wealthy man kept twenty cows for milking. He had six milkmaid slaves, and as was custom, used them as concubines. Tira brought us to his house and for a payment of a young mare, we used the women as we pleased.

Kristián, when you are with a group of young men of high spirits, it is easy to be led into behavior you would not otherwise do. Impulses often rule acts of young men. As you become a man, beware your unbridled lusts!

Those women were compliant as they must be, but not joyful. They endured our demands of their flesh. When we left, they prepared for the next morning's work.

During our ride back to my castle, Hrad Boleslav, Hněvsa suggested the three of them find me a permanent woman. Not a wife yet, but a consort, someone agreeable to give a man daily comfort, and perhaps an heir.

I admit a convenient female partner seemed like a good idea, though I may have been naïve enough to expect it to be an actual wife with a proper marriage sanctified by Dušan, and with a ceremony. There should be more to life with a woman than simply enjoying her body.

"And we must prepare you to be duke," Tuza told me.

***

Worshippers of the old religion in and around Prague learned not to display their faith openly. Many converted to Christianity, or pretended to. Others practiced their religion quietly, away from town. Some honestly kept both faiths, with a "double heart."

Dušan continued to hold ceremonies deep in the forest, near holy springs, or under ancient trees. His followers, and some were professed Christians, continued to come to him and his apprentice for aid as they had always done, with luck for a good harvest or to ease pain, and for his counsel.

I drew the crystal Dušan had given me from under my shirt and looked at the vein of gold. I too wanted counsel, to speak again with Dušan, my priest.

Václav had built a church dedicated to Svatý Vít. The king of the Franks wished to increase his influence over our people and had his bishop send some relics of the saint—bones from his hand—that were put in the new Church of Saint Vitus. They have been cherished here ever since. Václav would come to the church whenever he returned to Prague and give a thanksgiving prayer to the saint for the work he had done, for work he must complete, and for work he still had to begin.

When I visited Prague that time, Václav was away on a mission. He continued to travel the country and spread the Word. This was his primary goal—even above being duke, though his office gave him the power to do his Christian missions.

I passed the church on my way from the city to the east, seeking Dušan. It was sunset as I left Prague and entered the region of smoke, fire, and noise. This was the priest's domain, where he and his workers created iron metal from the earth's bones for tools and weapons.

His foreman Bratumil, with the single eyebrow, told me Dušan was visiting the charcoalliery further to the east of the city.

Bratumil, the boy slave captured with Podiven, had thrived in the ironworks and developed into a muscular worker, robust and happy in his labor, no longer a slave.

I walked past the forges themselves, my head ringing from the din of hammers, and through the shop space of iron workers. I'll describe the process, which you may not have learned.

They make the iron out of the earth by bringing ore to the works, driving horses pulling sledges piled with stone. The lumps of rock were rooted from the mine near the edge of an ancient bog nearly half a day's walk away. There the ore is roasted to cook moisture from it, and broken into fist-sized chunks. They load these onto another sledge and drag it to the forge.

Men pull the cooked ore off the dray and onto a large flat rock where the lumps are again broken into pieces the size of chicken eggs and loaded into baskets. Workers, bent from a lifetime of carrying their loads, heft them onto bearing shelves strapped to their backs and walk to the furnaces. These are chimneys made of molded clay about the height of a man, and many are in the shape of women.

Son, there is magic and ritual in ironmaking.

Workers, mostly slaves, may not eat certain foods while furnaces are hot, and cannot enjoy the company of women. The dangerous work requires full attention.

The hard, tedious labor of iron making is necessary for defense of our lands and our people, who like the ores, are drawn from the soil of Bohemia.

Young slave boys work enormous skin bellows that force air into the furnaces. They are often new to slavery, and probably thinking of families who sold them to cover debts, or who were killed or taken in warfare like the families of Podiven and Bratumil. Their bellows blow a consistent current of air into roaring furnaces. After some experience, their young muscles can work for hours in the heat. Sweat mixed with cinders and charcoal dust coats their bodies, nearly naked in that cool autumn evening. If they are not injured, the boys grow in strength and become bearers or miners, or if they show aptitude, they become forgers. Some sicken and die from fumes, dust, and labor.

When the time is right, forgers pull congealing iron "blooms" from the bottom of the furnace with heavy wooden rakes. The priest Dušan or his assistant Kamil examines the unshaped forms of red and white glowing matter, and the shape reveals the level of the iron's quality. The nature of iron can predict the success or failure of weapons in war, and perhaps the wars themselves.

They roll, drag and lift the hot masses onto the forging surface, large flat trunks of felled trees. Other men with great wooden mallets hammer the hot crumbly blooms and break off chunks of worthless slag to concentrate the congealing product of the furnaces: lumps of glowing red iron.

That bloom iron is heated again and beaten and hammered into more and more pure form.

The constant hammering of ore and the blooms, and working the iron, creates a constant rhythm of sound. It is nearly music, and pervades the realm of fire and fumes.

Iron is made into steel by heating it even hotter in special kilns and adding an exact ratio of charcoal to iron at an exact temperature, carefully timed, and pulled from the heat at the right moment.

They bring the hot metal to an anvil where one man holds it with tongs while two others beat it into rods with heavy hammers. They weld the rods together, an iron rod between higher-carbon steel rods, heated and beaten into shape. As it flattens, tongs turn it to its best side, and blows of hammer-men eventually shape it into a narrow flat form. It is reheated, then beaten more, and again, this time by a bladesmith working alone with a smaller steel hammer on an iron anvil.

Finally, when shaped like a sword or dagger, it is plunged into cool water to temper, then sharpened.

A tempered blade of good steel holds an edge, and when completed you hold in the palm of your hand weeks of the labors of a hundred men.

And like the crushed stones of ore, layered with a mass of charcoal and laid into the furnace's brilliant glow, our people have been through battles and invasions, fires and trials, and rendered into something strong.

This is the nature of your people, Kristián.

That day, my thoughts turned toward my meetings with my brother Václav, and then to the counsels of Hněvsa and Tuza. They each had plans and world views as well-structured as the constant rhythms of working iron. My view was as unshaped as the raw iron bloom drawn from the furnace.

I walked from the cacophonous forge to the charcoal pits and entered that realm of smoke, fog, and flame. I arrived at dusk, and it was like walking into another world.

A low roar from charcoal ovens created a sense of hidden power in the gloom.

Slaves worked the mounded pits, and young boys danced about like imps in the twilight. Plumes and billows of smoke rose from clay-covered pits of baking wood. A ghostly flame flared from the top of some vents, rich fumes burning with a greenish demon light.

Dušan's apprentice Kamil now managed the charcoal pits. He minded the times and signaled when to add fuel or open the vents, or smother the fires that bake finished charcoal.

The stench of cooking wood bent my mind into a dizzying haze as I paced through the place where slaves labored. It takes a lot of charcoal to fire the forges, to wrest tools and weapons from the stones of our land.

I was told by an older slave that Dušan and Kamil were taking some time to themselves in a field away from the smoke. I found them a short way from the pits beside a campfire. Others were tending the fire and cooking a meal.

Dušan's dog Král was there, and Dušan and his apprentice had each taken a woman to wife.

Women can be the best part of a man's life. Or, they can torment you into the most vile acts. You may never learn this because you will be a priest!

The two men were playing music.

Dušan played flutes as therapy for his people who were sore of heart, missing children or parents, people who were anguished, or distressed for other reasons. He would play a gentle tune on the wooden instrument he had made to soothe his patient, and with massage, herbal teas, and his good counsel, shared what gods revealed was their will.

Kamil's instrument differed from other flutes I had seen. It was extremely long, styled from his homeland far to the east, where Polish tribes live in old Moravia.

The mad oracle who tried to kill Dušan had bought Kamil from his parents there. She was a traveling magician and seer, and traded for him when he was nine years old. His family were poor sheep herders and lived in a district north of the ancient villages of Moravia. They played music there on a flute as tall as a man, a fujara, like the one Kamil played.

Traders who journeyed between cities of Bohemia and the east often came to see Dušan. Kamil asked them about the mystical flutes he remembered hearing as a child. One trader knew of these flutes, and with the skills of Dušan, helped Kamil craft one.

The traditional style of playing was unlike any other music heard in Czechia or anywhere else. Kamil had already learned from Dušan to play the flutes he made, and between them they re-created sounds made by the traditional fujara flute, until that time heard only by shepherds, their dogs and sheep on Moravian moors.

I stopped to view the scene of women cooking food, and the two men under a tree to the side playing their instruments in a tangled tune. Each struck a melody, the other matching and embellishing it, and after a few stanzas come around again to play a new melody based on the previous one, improvising a tune never heard before or since.

Dušan's high, lilting sound dominated the melodies. They were graced with popping notes of Kamil's long wooden instrument. The deep throbbing bass of the fujara flute was very emotive, and was as if the two of them could tell stories of the gods with nothing but wind.

Yes, this is the counsel I sought.

I walked up to the fire and, welcomed by the women, sat and listened to the music as it soothed my thoughts.

The couples shared with me their evening meal, a savory stew of lamb, turnips, garlic and millet, and afterward a pudding made from dried apples and honey. Grape wine ended the meal.

Kamil returned to the charcoal pits to monitor the progress of slaves, and I sat next to the priest who played on his flute a bit of an old hymn. At the end of his tune Dušan turned his focus to me, and seeing his caring face, I felt the entire world was ready to hear my burden.

Dušan's skills were so important to the commerce and strength of Prague that Václav did not press him on his faith, not much, though he apparently had an understanding with Václav about keeping the pagan services discreet. Václav's priest Erhard had shared with Dušan his observations of the Godly and peaceful ways of my brother, and that Václav honored the method his grandparents had learned of bringing the people to the Church gradually.

Dušan's gentle priestly ways conflicted little with the comforting words of Jesus spoken those centuries ago.

I shared my qualms with Dušan, my worries and fears of dark edges shading my future.

I told him I did not hate my brother.

I shared memories of Saskia, of Grandmother, and my shame for Mother when it was revealed at Václav's coronation that Veshtak's men—on orders from Dragomira—were the instruments of murder. The murder of Grandmother Ludmila.

I went into all that weighed on me, the women my friends and I had used, whispers that I should seize all power within my grasp and lever divisions of the people against themselves to win the throne.

I confessed I was unsure, that I could be consumed with thrills of sex and not concern myself with the woman I was using, or in the heat of a fight do what I needed to do to win at all costs, to strike my opponent twice for every blow he gave me, to pursue victory with no concern for any other thought—such as justness of my cause.

Then later, when alone in bed, I was haunted by ghosts of what Grandmother would have done. Or Václav. "Or what you, Dušan, would do," I said.

We were alone by the fire, and its fading glow cracked occasionally. A few sparks flew from the flames and chased each other into the stars above us, where souls of my father and Grandmother Ludmila lived.

Somewhere across the pastures, the mystical echo of Kamil's flute laid a thoughtful film of sound over the night. Král walked over to his master and lay by his side, looking up at him.

Dušan looked at me and then the stars.

"There are truths in the world, Boleslaw," he said.

"I believe that," I told him. "But I cannot place my feet on the right path."

After a thoughtful moment he said, "If you walk straight ahead on the wrong path, you will never reach your goal. And if with each step you turn to the right, or to the left, you will always go in a circle."

I waited.

He waited.

I finally said, "How do I find my path?"

He paused a moment, then opened his pouch and drew from it a black stone the size of his fist, a rough lump of black iron. It looked very heavy for its size.

Then he took a small wrought iron figure of a man from a pocket in his tunic. "Most men are drawn to the right path. It is in their nature."

He took the figure and moved it close to the stone, and released it. It jumped to the rock.

"This is a lodestone. I found it on top of the mountain, the heart of our land." I knew he meant the mountain Říp, where our ancient ancestor Czech, chief of our tribe, rested after leading his people from the east. They were looking for a new home, and Czech saw an omen, an eagle circling the hill, symbol of the great god Svantovít. He decided we should live here. It is the foundation story of our people.

"I made this figure of iron. See how it is drawn to the lodestone?" He pulled the doll away from the stone, let it go, and the tiny man again jumped to its magnetic pull.

"This lodestone is natural iron rock from Říp. When lightning strikes our mountain, the power of Svantovít goes into the rock, as it has gone into our land." He turned his face to the dying fire. "It has gone into you, as well, Prince Boleslav."

When a priest tells you the power of a god is within you, it gives you pause. Was he saying we are all priests?

"I must go sleep with my wife and keep her warm." Dušan went to his hut by the charcoal pits. He told his dog to remain with me.

I stayed by the fire, looking into its embers, trying to perceive a message from the gods.

Král stayed with me, sleeping warm by the fire until morning.

CHAPTER 6
Máj—The Time of Flowers

Duke Václav regularly traveled around his lands, sharing his laws and the words of Christ.

Podiven and the rest of the duke's retinue would pack horses and carry food and seeds and cuttings of plants. Václav shared the best types of crops for his people.

He saw to the planting of plum and other fruits, including grapes. His grandmother Ludmila had brought the vines to the Czechs, and Václav continued to improve their cultivation. He helped people in their harvests, to grind wheat into flour with the quern he carried, and to bake it into wafers representing the flesh of Christ in the service of mass.

Václav exemplified the Christian life, and converted many of his people to his religion by their witness of his good works and hearing the loving message of Jesus.

***

Despite the dark future I was letting myself be led into, I continued to hear confidences from my older brother.

Václav told me about one of his travels in spring. He woke from a night sleeping beneath the hovering stars of a clear sky, floating as in endless communion with the heavens.

He felt the presence of God.

He stood and saw a shining full moon surrounded by a hazy halo near the horizon, over an evening lake. Its reflection mirrored off the water's surface, and the scene displayed two great orbs and spangles of stars scattered in the sky and on the water. The vision he saw lay before him like an altar of many candles.

The duke walked forward. He stepped onto a trailway decked in gems of evening dew, and passed from forest to a field where sheep grazed quietly in predawn darkness.

It was the first of May, when animals and birds sing to each other and speak of love. Doves made soft calls, and scents of pine and sweet mosses filled the air.

Podiven woke to join him, to watch dawn begin to warm the misty horizon, lifting into a bluing sky.

They heard a faint sound through the flowering trees of a woman weeping, perhaps in a secret pain, hidden in the forest.

As they stepped out of the woods, the sun sent its first low beams of light onto the sacred lake, where they penetrated the surface and lit the waters and fish below. Václav turned his eyes around the horizon to see tips of huge beech trees reaching upwards as if to embrace the growing light of day, and eagles spiraled above.

Light grew, and a distant shepherd waved his hand in greeting. Václav replied, and saw far to his left a gray-robed figure retiring into the forest by an enormous oak. The crying woman?

Podiven and Václav turned to see her better, her gown flowing in an early morning zephyr, and they saw bleached remains of an executed criminal, a scattering skeleton lashed to an instrument of punishment, a breaking wheel. The bones were broken in many places, and his fleshless head gazed up at the sky, his mouth open as if begging heaven for mercy.

Freshly picked flowers lay below the shattered skeleton.

The woman stopped at the wood's edge and returned her gaze to the bones on the wheel. She saw the lost future of herself and her lover. A glint of early morning sunbeam flashed from a tear streaking down her cheek, and she turned back to shadows of the wood, back to her dark sorrow.

As she left the field in its morning gloaming, a falling star streaked across the sky's far western dimness.

Václav and Podiven stood, and then knelt in the early sun-glow of the lightening day. They prayed for the soul of this criminal who had died so piteously.

Yet—the woman had brought flowers in remembrance.

The wind stroked the grasses around them where they knelt. Václav told me a bird, a crested tit, fluttered to land on the wheel by the skull. The bird trilled its zee-zee-zee-zee song as my brother prayed.

And he had a revelation he knew came from God: Cruelty is not justice.

✳✳✳

The rest of Václav's camp woke and prepared for another day of travel.

Václav and his retinue went to a nearby village and found lodging at a monk's cabin. After helping the monk complete his chores they ate and prayed by his hearth. Then the monk told him the tale of young Jarmila and her lover, the criminal executed on the wheel.

The breaking wheel is well known as a tool of punishment for murderers or those who commit serious crimes. The condemned is staked to the ground, and the heavy wheel is rolled over him to crush arms and legs; or he is tied to the wheel and an executioner strikes and breaks his bones with an iron rod. Death often comes days afterward in most public agony.

Years earlier, lords of the nearby town often went into the countryside and sowed their wild seed, as I did with Tuza and Tira before I became duke. Often, while hunting boar or deer, they encountered a lonely hut in the hills or in the wild forest. If there were women, they would, as we have done, sport with them—whether willing or not. "Sport" is often not really a good term for this.

On one such hunt, the son of a nobleman and his fellows came upon a young woman gathering honey from her hives. Her father was away among his flock, and the man seized her and roughly relieved his lust in her, then continued his hunting outing.

Nine months later she bore a child from his seed, unknown to the young man who had raped her.

She named the baby boy Vilém.

The boy grew up unfathered, or rather raised by the shepherd, his village, and the woman who bore him. He had woodsmen and foresters as his family, and they learned of his natural abilities. He took up the hunting bow and spear. Because of his talents and his kind nature, he eventually became a leader among young people he knew and was called "Lord of the Forest." He was admired by all, and he especially showed his attentions to the young girl Jarmila, oldest daughter of a woodsman friend.

Vilém brought game he had hunted for the father and daughter to eat, and to her he also brought flowers. Together they walked trails and pathways in the sacred forest and shared the joy of love amid the fireflies of midsummer, tiny candles to guide their way. The breezes in the trees were lullabies to their pleasure.

The young noble who had fathered the hunter became lord himself and continued his intemperate ways. Though older, he was still strong in his passions. While roving again, he spied the young Jarmila at her labors while her father and Vilém were at the hunt.

He took the girl, and despite her pleas, raped her, as he had the mother of her lover those years earlier.

Vilém heard her weeping cries and ran to her with his hunting spear. At the sight of his woman in distress he ran his lance though the attacker's body, his blood father, and watched him die as the lord's men grasped his attacker. They, more than their master, knew Vilém's parentage. They carried him back to the town with the body of their chief.

Vilém was soon tried and condemned as a parricide, killer of his own father. He was sentenced, and they broke him on the wheel. For two days, he suffered the most extreme agony before he finally choked his last breath.

They carried his body, still lashed to the wheel, to the hill near where he lived. In time it became as Václav found it, pecked by birds, gnawed by foxes, bones scattering, settling to the soil where all flesh must someday return.

And his faithful lover Jarmila returns to Vilém when she can, to lay fresh flowers at the sunny open grave of her lost hope.

The tale had a devastating effect on Václav. A hero's justifiable murder of a fiend was punished with a prolonged and excruciating public execution.

Harsh punishments are nothing new. A man who had stolen another man's sheep could lose his home and be driven from his land to die of hunger on the road, or if he were important, we could lock him in a pit for months. Sentences for serious crimes could mean loss of an eye, or fingers from a hand, or more commonly, ears. Of course, for murder the sentence was usually death, no matter the circumstances.

Well, as I have seen, I suppose some circumstances do matter.

Anyway, Václav took the kindness of Christian scriptures to his heart.

He made a point of going to trials of criminals to witness testimonies and judgements. Several times he overruled a decision he thought too harsh, and he codified and changed how courts mete out justice. He remembered his revelation from God while he was in the woods: Cruelty is not Justice. Under my brother's rule, courts became more merciful, and punishments standardized across the land. Sentences of mutilation were reduced, as were executions.

When a proper capital judgement was to be given, Václav would leave the courtroom to have no hand in killing of a man, even if law demanded it.

Many—maybe most—people thought the reform of courts improved society, the way we treated each other, and they were pleased. I have kept those reforms under my rule.

But others believed in forms of traditional punishments, in vengeance, and this dissatisfaction was shared among the brutal followers of Veshtak.

CHAPTER 7
Říjen—The Month of Rutting Passion

At the suggestions of his friends and his boyars—and myself, my brother took a woman in consort. The woman was, as our traditions were then, not a formal wife, but could bear him an heir. Formal marriages were not common except as contracts for property. He could marry later, when a good tribal alliance could be made by the union.

His consort was named Agata, sixteen years old, a good age to begin bearing children. She was a local girl from south of Prague, and already properly experienced with men. Agata was the daughter of a shepherd. She had two sisters, so her father was wealthy in daughters, and he was well compensated.

Václav had followed the Church's strictures as he interpreted them regarding sexual relations and abstained all his life, until his boyars and friends convinced him he must produce an heir for the good of the royal line.

He told me later he prayed about this union, and he and Agata—who was not really interested in religion—spent hours praying in the chapel before their nights in bed together.

Václav was so moved by the physical experience with Agata and her ability to so thoroughly please him that he had an epiphany from God during the act. Now, I enjoy a good frolic as much as anyone, but he told me his experience was "as if I had opened the gate of heaven and stepped a foot briefly inside. Pleasure and thrill overwhelmed me, beyond what I deserve in this life."

He did not think it was proper to experience such extreme pleasure this side of death, and thought it was his duty to repeat the physical union only until Agata became pregnant. When it became evident an heir was coming, he gathered the strength of his resolve and forbade himself any further intercourse. He told her, "I will be a brother to you, and you will be a sister to me."

A son was born, named Izbrjaslav, meaning "One Chosen for Fame." As Václav's heir, he should someday become duke.

Three months after the child was born, Agata became restless. Now, it may be very well for a monkish Christian duke to subvert natural urgings to his interpretation of God's will, but it is something else for a lusty country girl with a thirst for fun and human touch.

Frequently, while Václav was in the chapel or away on his missions, Agata took the baby for outings and saw people in town. Václav's page and friend Podiven often observed her when he was not with his master, and she observed him as well, a tall and vital young man. He was loyal to his duke, and pious, but he was human and of the earth, like most everyone.

Such things happen.

The two walked to the palace and placed the sleeping baby in his crib. Then they fell into each other's arms, finding such joy as is possible in this world, though shadowed by black guilt.

Václav discovered their tryst, and true to his nature, after days of prayer, he blessed their union. My brother hosted Podiven and Agata in a Christian wedding ceremony, with Václav remaining "brother" to both of them. He gave her hand to Podiven, and he gifted her jewelry— rings to hang from her temples to frame her face.

Václav himself, as is now traditional, bound their wrists together, and placed a spoon in their hands. They must share their life's work, symbolized by finding a way to share in eating dumpling, beef, and onion stew while bound this way.

And so, by his blessing, the couple's love for my brother grew even stronger.

✳✳✳

Beyond cutting wood and helping plant and harvest, Václav, when he was able, bought slaves from traders of Prague, and converted them to

Christianity. His kind gentleness was inspirational to people. His Christian actions and meekness made him universally loved, or nearly so.

In his travels Václav built many churches and dedicated shrines. He consecrated sacred sites and pulled down the old religion's shrines and monuments, and this brought resistance and resentment from some.

The priest Veshtak heard of this.

***

Václav decided he should follow the biblical stricture of "Honor thy Father and thy Mother," and brought Mother Dragomira back from Croatia. Personally, I didn't see how this could help anything. By then, everyone knew she arranged the murder of Grandmother Ludmila.

Mother moved near me, near where I built my castle. She had conversations with Tuza and his brother Tira, with Veshtak, and especially with the father of Hněvsa.

When I was nearing my eighteenth birthday, the sons of Tunna came to see me.

Tuza said, "Boleslav, it is time to begin living as a full man."

Now Tuza had a very good idea of what he meant, to be a "full man." For him, it meant using all his power, all his abilities, talents, friendly connections, and position to achieve all worldly gain for himself. And expanding on that, for his family and friends, those who could benefit him and help to achieve even more for himself. This is a very common philosophy in the world.

Who was I at that age to say it is wrong?

Tuza and Tira, Veshtak and Hněvsa had all benefitted from the friendship of my mother, and from me. They were not friends with the duke, my brother. I was their friendly connection to the ruling house.

Václav divided his lands and gave me half to rule over, though he was my duke and I was tributary to him.

I believed our people needed a strong and fortified castle to be built where I ruled, for protection from warring enemies. I had a home two days' journey to the east of Prague, on a hill across the Jizera River. It is a land rich in honey and vineyards, herds of cattle, sheep and goats, where an island allows easy fords when the water is not high.

Trade routes passed near here, to Prague, and to Mělník, then Zittau in the Frankish lands, and another to Polish lands and beyond.

That location is a good place for a stronghold. It could eventually link Prague and Budeč and other forts into a defensible chain of iron, binding and protecting our land.

Tuza convinced me I should have a castle built in the Roman fashion, an enclosed stone structure instead of our traditional wall on a hilltop, or a wooden castle like others in Bohemia. The people did not want to build my fortress there because they did not see a need for such a castle, and they were busy harvesting their millet.

Tuza said, "You should have a castle that can be a citadel and will show your strength. Not something everyone else has," meaning a wooden castle like my brother lived in. "You should have a modern castle, one befitting a king!"

Back in earlier days, everyone in Bohemia—even the duke—worked in the fields and did other labor. When a duke is crowned, the farmer-boots of our ancestor Přemysl are displayed to him to remind him even the duke had an ancestor who was a common worker. The people accepted the duke as leader, but they expected the duke to guide and support the people, not order his wishes on them.

Tuza told me that was wrong. Dukes and princes were above ordinary workmen. We should never labor. Our job was to hunt, learn swordcraft, produce heirs, and make war. He said, "That is strength! The strength of command!"

Tuza's father Tunna was from the Frankish lands to the north. There, dukes and kings rule over the lords, and lords rule the peasants. In Czechia our system was not so strict.

A council of village headmen was called for me to tell them about building my new castle.

These meetings were usually called to discuss what was best for the people, and the duke heard plans and chose from among them, then facilitated the beneficial work.

This time the area's leaders reluctantly gathered to hear what I would demand of them. I was barely eighteen and still learning how a man should act. Tuza, older now, was willing to guide me.

At Tuza's suggestion I described the stone castle I wanted, where it must be located, and the schedule for its construction. My friends Hněvsa, Tira and Tuza stood in back of the meeting and watched.

The headmen were tired from their harvesting labors and wanted to return to their fields before weather ruined their crops.

One of them, a dignified and grandfatherly man, stood and told me, "We do not need another castle now. The gord fort on the hill of Roztoky has served us well and can serve us again. If a danger arises, we will build a wood fort for defense." He sat down, so others could have a say.

Councils often had disagreements, and there was a give-and-take among leaders that eventually led to compromise, or a decision all could live with. But Tuza's attitude about rule had its effect on me.

Tuza shot me a quizzical look, as if asking what I would do next.

"This is my plan. This is where the stone castle will be built!" I said this too loudly, perhaps nervously, because the headman who had answered me chuckled.

I recalled the words of Tuza, that this council and my acts here will determine how I would be seen as a leader, how I would rule my lands.

"You are not our duke," said the headman. "I am leaving this council." He stood, and the rest stood with him.

I could feel the eyes of Tuza and of my friends boring into me as I stood up. I felt a rush of blood in my face.

I stepped toward the man, and in one movement, swept my sword Tvůrce Králů from its sheath. With strength of excitement, my body moved as I had trained it over the past decade. In one blow I struck the head from the old man.

I stepped back as his body fell. The head thumped on the stone pavement, sounding like a fish being chopped. The body relaxed, fell, and made a sputtering sound as it exhaled. Warm blood ran over my feet.

Kristián, I see my cruel act startles you. I, too, was startled. Shocked, even. This was the first man I had ever killed. Alas, not the last!

For a moment, I could not take my eyes off of the waste of the man. Then I turned my gaze to the townspeople's faces, and they were afraid. I lifted my chin and breathed deeply, smelling their fear, feeling my power. I glanced at my friends, and their eyes were the size of goose eggs. Tuza smiled and nodded.

I looked again at the people, and they did not return my gaze. My body thrilled.

"You will build my stone castle," I commanded. "You will bring all your boys and men. Come at sunrise in three days and build it to my plan. Now go! And get this body from this place!"

I turned and walked from the square. My knees were like butter and felt tremulous, but I paced steadily. Hněvsa quickly stepped up to my side and with matching strides, we went to his house to clean blood from my shoes.

My ears were ringing with the sound of my own rushing blood.

Later that evening, while Tuza met with Veshtak, Tira and Hněvsa joined me in a pot of mead. Hněvsa congratulated me on my firm actions. Yet I heard a small voice in my mind asking what would become of the man's family, and if I was right to kill the tired old farmer for such a reason, perhaps vainglorious, of building a new stone castle we really didn't need yet.

"They will listen to you now, Boleslav!" said Hněvsa. "You have taken power, and they will never question your orders again!" He laughed and the three of us drank, though Tira remained silent.

I wished I could speak to Dušan about what I had done and my feelings about it. But that night I put on a brave face and joined them, seeking the flagon's bottom.

In months to come, the castle slowly rose. The people worked for me for ten days, beginning each full moon, weather permitting, until the castle was complete.

***

And then I took a wife—or at least a consort.

I treated her well. She was a daughter of a well-off farmer near my castle. I gave her father a cow and a bull, and took his daughter back to Hrad Boleslav.

She was glad to come. She was fifteen years old and eager to begin her life as a woman. Zivanka was her name, meaning "Lively," and it suited her. We were together for four years, and she bore me your sister, and your older brother, young Boleslav.

My next wife was your mother, Biagota. I married her to form an alliance with a duke of Bulgaria. The gold and cattle tribute we pay to the Franks is oppressive, and I tried to build an alliance to resist it, but it didn't work. We still pay.

When your mother and I got married, I had gold denar coins struck with our names and faces on them, the first coinage of our people. She liked that. We do what we can to please our women.

Cloths of value were not much good except in Prague, and even here a silver or gold coin is easier to place a value on.

Biagota didn't like Ivanka in the house, so after one more night of her lively company, I let her go. She was ready to move on as well, I think. Four years seems like a long time for a young woman to be with the same man. She found a home with a friend closer to her father's home south of my castle. Our children stayed in my household, of course.

When your older brother Boleslav was born, I at last had a son and heir. I felt life was going well for me. My fields and flocks were increasing, and the people had food that lasted through the winters, mostly.

But I need to get back to my story.

***

The priest Veshtak was in and out of our area for years, traveling to the land of Poles and of Croats. Tuza kept in touch with him, and he met with Mother too, though her attitude toward him was changing. I could see it when they were together.

Mother's time with the Croats had given her space to look back on her life.

She had mellowed, if you can believe it, of someone like her.

Dragomira still loved power, the attraction of it like iron to a dark lodestone. But she also had seen sorrow, and she even spoke with Václav's priest, Erhard, from time to time.

I think the murder of Grandmother Ludmila haunted her, as well as the shadow of what was to come.

CHAPTER 8
Září—A Blazing Glow

Summer had mostly passed, and cool breezes moved the leaves remaining on the trees. They now turned yellow and golden in the early autumn air. Bright linden leaves that reflected sunlight carpeted the forest floor. Their glow lit the trunks and limbs of sacred groves from beneath.

My wife Biagota was nearing her time for the delivery of my second son. It would be near the end of September, so the celebration of your birth was to be on the Christian holiday of Saints Cosmas and Damian, the martyred Christian apothecaries. It is said they never charged for their medicines, and they impressed many to the Faith. They were killed by a Roman emperor's soldier centuries ago—tortured on crosses, stoned, shot with arrows, and finally beheaded when they would not recant their faith.

Such bloody deaths are the fate of saints.

So, we celebrate their day, the same as the pagan holiday of Dožínky, the autumn equinox—the anniversary of Grandmother Ludmila's murder.

My friend Hněvsa now ruled his house, as his father was old and in his dotage. He invited me to bring Biagota to his castle, to birth our child—you, Kristián. Hněvsa had good midwives, one Christian and one of the old religion, both well versed in the knowledge of Kazi, the herb-wise mistress of ancient history.

He would hold the feast celebrating your birth. Tuza and Tira and other friends would be there with their wives and consorts, and Veshtak.

I was to invite my brother the duke as well.

Václav continued his missions of promoting Christ's message in the lands. He and his page walked pathways through sacred forests that our people had venerated for countless generations. They passed people in groves, perhaps an older peasant carrying a bundle of firewood on his back, who paused and bowed such as he could as the prince passed. They met wary travelers who gave any strangers encountered wide passage. He met them all with a joy, good humor and Christian greeting they did not forget. The nymphs, ogres and fairies of our land's lore did not reveal themselves to this traveling missionary.

Wherever Václav went, he continued his good works and charities and benefitted our country each year with better yields of grains, fruit, honey, and cattle.

Honey is important to our land, and your tutor might not have told you about it.

Every year beekeepers build skeps for their bee hives and set them out empty. They gather swarming honeybees and bring them to colonize the skeps.

They make skeps of woven reeds, coiled into a basket. The skep is inverted and an opening in the hive lets bees in and out to do their work.

When the hive is full of honey, smoke is pushed into it, and the skep is cut in two. Smoke makes the bees sleepy while their hive is destroyed. The beekeeper scoops chunks of honeycomb out into bowls where it is crushed and separated from beeswax. The crushed wax is soaked in water, and they make mead from the honey water. We use beeswax for candles and other purposes. But the hive is destroyed when the honey and wax are harvested.

Václav created and shared a type of chamber, a box within the skep that preserves a queen bee and permits the beekeeper to move a nucleus of her hive to a new skep. By saving a queen bee and some workers, bee colonies survive to grow anew, even though the old hive in the skep is lost. Saving hives increases the number of colonies beekeepers can maintain each year and increases yield, better for the farmer and for our land.

Our people were always grateful to Václav and admired his strong, selfless ways, his basic charity of nature—even if they didn't immediately convert to his religion. When he told them he was following the teachings of Jesus, many became Christian because of his pure example of good will.

I suppose if he told them he was following Mohammed's example, they would have become followers of that faith.

I have learned most people are drawn to do good for each other—though not all. The most revered prophets put their goodness into words, and the most successful of them write it down.

But there were always some who reject new ideas, and Tuza and Veshtak encouraged them for their own purposes.

Rumors of Tuza and Veshtak's plans had made their way to Prague, and Duke Václav had sent for Christian warriors to guard the castle when he was away from the city. He sent a plea to Budeč, and had his priest, Erhard, write to some faithful among the Danes. These were Christians whose fathers had been converted by a missionary named Ansgar, of whom you may have heard. Twenty of these crusading men came to guard the palace.

The Danes were tall and strong-looking. They carried arms of different form than what we Czechs wore. Many in their lands still worshipped the old gods, but those at Prague Castle were dedicated Christians, fanatical in their defense of the religion. They offered themselves to service as crusaders. Their language was strange and incomprehensible to me, but they were admirable in their reverence and habits. They did not live in our country long enough to leave a strong influence on the people.

Václav would not cease his travels, but replied to me he would take time from his mission work to visit us and celebrate your birth, Kristián.

***

Hněvsa told me to leave arrangements up to him and to go hunting wild boar with Tuza and Tira. I think he did this to distract me from considering what we were planning for Václav.

The three of us and our party hunted game for about ten days. We ventured deep into the forests of our land. Our group included five men for setting up camp and taking care of our horses and dogs, and pack animals for our hunting weapons, food and wine.

Several times we came to settlements where we could find willing farmers' wives and daughters. Well, looking back, I see they had no choice, and their men were driven from these homesteads while we were there. I regret that now, my causing such anguish to anyone.

The hunt was unsuccessful on the first day. Our scout found a boar trail, but the dogs found no fresh scent until the second day, when the hounds voiced they had bayed an animal.

The three of us spurred our horses to the spot, and the dogs, seasoned enough to know not to actually attack the boar, kept lively and harried it in place against a wall of rock. A slave handed me a lance.

Tuza dismounted and walked toward the beast. He called, "Spear him, Boleslav! He's yours!"

I lifted the spear and felt its weight as the boar grunted in fear. It feinted a charge at the hounds, and Tuza threatened it back to the wall with his spear.

I'd killed many boars. This was not as large as some. I didn't see it as a challenge, really. But he was cornered, wide-eyed, dangerous. I hesitated, then steeled myself.

I called to the hounds, and they began barking and lunging about at the boar.

I lifted the spear, straight and solid ash wood, pointed with hard iron, sharpened to cut flesh.

The thought of cutting flesh made me pause again. My brother was of flesh.

"Now, Boleslav!" cried Tira.

I regained my thoughts and rocked on my feet until my balance matched the best timing for the thrust, and I drove the blade's tip in the side behind the shoulder and felt the long blade slide into the hog's organs, stopped by the spearhead's quillon. The pig's shriek of pain and fear rang through the forest. It rang through me.

**

That night around the fire we shared our stories of the day's hunt, and when I turned our talk to the upcoming birth of my next child and the festivities, my fellows turned our conversation back to the hunt, and what we might expect on the next day.

The following morning we pursued a buck into the trees and Tira and his brother outpaced me, chasing the hounds. I took a wrong turn, and in a few heartbeats found myself in an open glade, alone.

Sounds of birds misted from the woods.

On one end of the clearing was a muddy bog, where animals had tracked to find water. I walked my horse into dappled sunlight that spattered the grassy area where deer had fed.

My horse was restless, sensing something I could not.

I believe there are no dragons, at least not in the world now, not here. But there was something…

I dismounted and put my hand on my sword "Kingmaker," not the lance I would employ to spear a bear or a boar, or on the bow and quiver I used to shoot a hart.

There was something threatening. Not game, but something… some challenge.

I recall my experience was of things happening slowly, as if in a dream.

I had a sense of the drones of pipes, or perhaps the low tones of Kamil's fujara flute.

My mount spirited about the clearing, just forty paces wide, starting, snorting and jumping at each shadow from the underbrush. He shook and sidled to the center of the clearing, and there in the middle of the wild pasture glade, open to Svantovít's sky, was a small woven panel about as wide as a handsbreadth, made of white, skinned twigs. In the center were interlaced black feathers of a carrion crow.

As I bent to pick it up, a cloud passed over the sun, leaving me in deep shadow. I stood to gaze upward.

I looked to the sky and saw a high-flying bird against the darkness, an eagle. An omen, as of our ancient ancestor Czech? What might this portend to me? Was Svantovít calling?

Dušan had told me, "Men are drawn to their paths."

The eagle called, and it soared and dived, then called again, and in a flash was gone.

The high clouds boiled.

I looked down again at the woven talisman. I dropped it and stepped away.

My horse was calmer now, and with quieting words, I mounted him. He bent his head down to munch on grass. I reached into my shirt and grasped the crystal amulet Dušan had given me. As he had said, it had no power of itself, but it was a familiar token of him and gave me some peace. When I saw the black feathers, I suspected they could foretell—I knew they foretold an evil deed, and death.

Quiet, save the birdsong. Yet the glade seemed to hum with indistinct distant bagpipes, or the low notes of a flute.

I looked about me and saw several traces and tracks leading from the clearing into the forest. To what path was I drawn?

Even then, I was beset with horrors.

I knew my own mother had ordered the murder of my gentle grandmother Ludmila.

I looked at my hands and in horror, recognized them as tools that must kill my good brother.

In that still glade I listened to the quiet hum of bees, a whisper of leaves above me rustling in a breeze. I looked up and as the cloud passed to let the sun shine on me again, I saw deep blue sky dappled with a pattern of clouds and a flight of white storks sailing to the west, like souls fleeing the earth.

I wondered what Dušan would read of these. Or what Veshtak would see.

I realized what mattered is what I saw.

I tried to order my thoughts, and the pattern emerging of the near future was not good. I felt swept onward by currents drawing me into what would happen, without the ability to change my path. I realized I did not have the strength of resolve to alter it—the strength of Václav!

The sound of a distant hunting horn called. Tira's.

I took a few deep and tremulous breaths. Did I want to return to the hunt, the society of these men and their plans? Would it not be best to lose myself in the forest and live in a cave, taking my own counsel until my time of danger was past and my way was made clear?

Again, I heard the horn call.

After a moment's pause, I raised my horn and winded a blast. In a short time one of our hounds appeared in my quiet glade and pranced about, a happy servant seeking his master's favor.

"Go!" I commanded, and the gleeful dog leapt into a trail back to Tuza and Tira, one I could follow on my mount.

In my weakness I returned to a path I had not sought.

***

The day of the feast was upon us.

My party returned to Hněvsa's settlement with two hogs for the feast. I moved in a fog, and passed my horse to the grooms.

I paced through the grounds, past the granary and stables, children gadding about, their parents carrying food and goods for the party.

My way was laid before me, Kristián.

I would kill my brother, take his crown, and lead my people into… the future.

What future was this? A future of the past? Where brutal kings kill their relatives to gain and hold power? It has happened often enough!

Biagota was no longer in her birthing prime, past thirty-three years of age, yet she was happy. Joyful even, envisioning the birth of another child, a daughter who could be parlayed into an alliance, or a son—a warrior for our people.

Or one who could save my soul, Kristián!

I sometimes wished I was a common man, just tending his apiaries, his orchards, his flock. There would be no intrigue, no hidden words or stealthy plots, just a laborious day's work, honest sweat, and then home to a meal and the welcoming body of my wife, to the world's goodness the gods have given us. Perhaps this is not a realistic look at the life of common people. A raiding party could come from nowhere and kill us all.

But Kristián, we are born princes, and our fates lead to other destinies.

***

I later heard that one of Hněvsa's Christian servants went to Václav and his traveling party before they arrived in the village. He warned my brother he was to be killed at this feast. Václav smiled and spoke of "God's will." His party rode into the castle grounds.

On the days of celebration there were games and challenges, contests of strength and speed, of archer and spearman and blade-throwing. Flutes and drums kept a lively noise in the background.

There were some Christians among the attending crowd, but most followed the old ways. Religion is one thing, custom is another. Oh, perhaps not, perhaps not.

The event was ostensibly a feast for Christian Saints Cosmas and Damian, but it was also the "equal day" of pagans, halfway between winter and summer solstices, harvest festival time, so both religions celebrated the day of this feast.

Václav's traveling party arrived before sundown, and some of his men joined in the tournaments.

Hněvsa's castle staff were mostly not Christian, though some were, and kept their worship privately among themselves. More than a few had been converted by Václav himself on his travels, and were quietly loyal to him. Some remembered our grandmother, Ludmila.

A horn sounded, a signal the roasting meat was ready and guests should move inside.

The great feast was laid, and more guests arrived. Boars and pigs roasted, a whole deer was on a massive spit, fine pastries on trays, like scores of little baked wheels with cherries and poppy seeds, sweet and crunchy. Great jugs of mead, beer and wine were poured into partyers' cups, and horns.

I gave Václav a place of honor near me, of course, and his alert page Podiven sat beside him. Podiven's wife and Václav's heir remained in Prague.

Veshtak was there, with his lion-mane face. Tira and Tuza were there, and another pagan priest, short and wizened, with only one eye. He giggled in cackling laughter.

The father of Hněvsa had grown old and grizzled. He was well into his seventh decade, the old shepherd, and though diminished physically, he still had some power of words over his son.

Tuza sat near me with one of his consorts at his arm. She was happy at the man's attention and displayed her silver and lead temple rings similar to those Václav had given Podiven's bride Agata. Tira sat with his woman, somberly looking about the reveling hall as if in foreboding.

Men made speeches, shouted above the din. They praised me for fathering a third child, "Manly strength!" they cried, though to me producing a child seems more the mother's strength than the male's, whose total duty in the affair was purely pleasure.

The feasting fire blazed warm, and its roaring light and lamps made the room bright and lively.

Just after the servers left my table, one of the serving girls helping the midwives came into the hall and told me the birth would be soon, before morning. I thanked her and gave her a pat on her behind as she returned to my wife's company. On her way out of the hall she stopped to glance and smile at her duke, who gave her a wave before turning back to his meal.

The duke was not prone to drink in excess, though that evening he consumed more wine than during a day full of communion services. He seemed to glow with a look of a blessed man, satisfied with the moment.

One man who Tuza had brought had fallen deep into his mead horn. He stood on unsteady legs. He pulled a dagger from his belt and reeled toward Václav, but Podiven stood and blocked him. His left hand dashed the blade from the grip of the drunken would-be assassin, and his right fell like one of Dušan's hammers onto his head. Servants carried his senseless body from the hall.

Podiven shot Václav a warning glare, which my brother discounted with a smile and a reassuring wave of his hand. Perhaps the wine influenced him that night.

Earlier than most, Václav decided to retire, as the party was devolving into raucous and lascivious songs and behavior which offended his Christian morality. He was weary from his travel and heavy with food. He, Mstena and Podiven left the noisy hall.

As they walked to their room, another servant of Hněvsa approached them through the dark hallway. He spoke with wide eyes in the shifting light from the candle and warned the duke again of plans for his murder. He had a horse prepared for him, and Václav could leave that instant to safety beyond the walls, and from there to the sanctuary of the forest, and to Prague.

Václav blessed him, of course, and despite Podiven's and Mstena's urgings, he continued to his chamber. They went to bed and slept deeply.

***

As usual, the duke awoke before sunrise, before anyone else in his company.

He recalled the night before and sought to pray for souls of the party's attendees. To me, his brother, and my newborn son, his nephew. He went to pray for us!

He went to pray for you, Kristián. You were born while we were reveling.

Václav rose without disturbing his servants. He crept through the sleeping compound to the chapel, where he would kneel before the altar and give himself to the peace of prayer while his host and his fellows still slept.

But I also had risen early.

I saw him quietly treading the cool pavement to the chapel, to sanctuary with his god.

Tuza and Tira were standing by me. We knew he would be up early to pray, and we planned to meet him. Hněvsa and two of his men were across the plaza in shadows.

Now was the moment.

I was frozen. I could not move. I sweated in the night air's coolness and loosened my shirt.

Tuza nudged me. I did not respond. I heard the blaring drone of a shepherd's pipe in my head, which I am sure no one else heard.

Tuza drew my sword from my scabbard and placed it into my hand.

"Now, Boleslav. Now is your time."

I did not move. The tone in my head was so loud.

Tuza pushed me and I stepped from the predawn shadow of a wall. Václav saw me.

He stopped. "Hello, Brother," he said quietly. "You were a gracious host to us last evening."

My world was spinning.

This was not an unexpected act I was to commit. They had trained me all my life for this moment. Not in an overt, "You will kill your brother!" statement. Everything was implied, suggested. But I always knew this moment would come.

I moved without directive, as if blown by the wind, without thinking.

I raised my arm to strike him, and as I had been trained for a decade, I brought the blade of Kingmaker down on my brother's head.

But my stroke was weak. At the last instant I turned the blade forged by Dušan, wrought by Kamil, finished and sharpened by Bratumil, and it hit my brother, my beloved, brilliant, holy and revered saint of a brother, with the flat of the blade on his forehead.

I stood aghast, that I could raise my hand to strike Václav, my duke, who had carried on the work of Grandmother Ludmila, and strengthened our land, made it more wealthy, more Christian. Under my brother's watch, it was a wonderful land, growing in peace, forcing back primitive ignorance.

I had struck my brother.

He staggered.

My sword clattered to the pavement, and I stepped backwards, tripped, fell.

I lay on the stones in miserable despair, my black future in my mouth, as were my tears and bile, and I sobbed in shame. I who was to be duke!

Václav bent and picked up my sword. "Kingmaker."

He bowed to offer it back to me. "In love, brother, let us not kill this day."

And as I drew myself to my knees and looked up into my brother's gentle and smiling face, he seemed to radiate a holy light. I will never forget the warm look of his kind eyes on me in that moment. He had glory about him.

Then the others came.

My friends had heard the action, Tuza and Tira, and Hněvsa and his men.

"Strength, Boleslav. This is your hour!" cried Tuza.

"Duke Boleslav!" cried Hněvsa.

The duke looked up and saw figures springing from shadows. He saw he was outmanned. He turned to run toward the chapel door— locked on my orders!

Hněvsa lunged at the unarmed duke and swung down his sword to strike him on the arm.

Tuza charged at my wounded brother and hacked down on his shoulder, like the blows that killed our father.

"Brother!" I cried, as Hněvsa's sword ran him through, as his hand clutched the handle of the chapel door. "Brother! Václav!"

Another blow from Tuza dealt him death, and Václav fell in his own free flowing blood.

I could not move. The starry heavens descended upon me and pinned me to the flagstones.

Tira stood next to me.

Not to be unsure of the result of their attack, Hněvsa and Tuza cut his body to pieces, and Václav's blood washed over the stones. It flowed toward me, a trickle of holy crimson. It touched my right hand, and its warmth burned.

In pain and despair I looked up at the fading stars above and wondered if I could ever find a place in that array, with my father, with my grandmother, with the blessed. With Václav—and the pieces of his body still warm.

Tira helped me struggle to my feet, and we stood in the gloom together.

Damned! I could not speak. Tira stood by me in silence.

Hněvsa approached me and said, in almost a whisper, "You are duke now, Boleslav."

An icy breeze drifted through the plaza. It burned my ears, stung my nostrils.

I looked at Václav's blood on my fingers and wiped it on the front of my tunic. I felt the heat from Václav over my heart.

I feel it still, Kristián.

Twelve years later I still feel the heat of that stain, Václav's holy blood over my heart. Sometimes it warms, but more often it burns.

Tuza wiped his blade and his hands. He turned his bright eye to me and said, "Let us go kill Dragomira now! You can mourn her and your brother at the same time!"

I could not speak. Tira held his hand on my shoulder.

In the distance I could see the chapel priest hovering about the side of the building, feared of coming into the open, to such sacrilege!

Hněvsa called his serving men and several of them came to him bearing arms. He gave the order to put to blade all of Václav's party, and they scattered to rooms held by Podiven, Mstena and the others.

Tuza gathered his allies, and they prepared their horses. Cries of woe and pain echoed from walls and through the halls and alleys of Hněvsa's great house.

The skittish Christian priest came when Tira called him, and he opened the chapel. Tira led me in. I tread gently on the stones by the small building dedicated to Jesus, Prince of Peace. This was the room where Václav meant to come for morning vespers.

"Tira," I said.

"Yes, Your Grace," he answered. His tone did not hold irony at my new title, yet his words were a shameful rebuke.

I asked, "Tira, what have I done?" He looked at me with eyes of great hurt and shame.

The priest lit a candle and began a chant, not of celebration, but of sorrow, penance. In the early hour in that small church I felt the weight of intense and unholy shame.

The priest quietly left to gather up the quarters and body pieces of my brother. He still lay scattered outside in the glow of new dawn.

In that moment I realized what a dreadful feast day this had been, that saints' day, the birth of my son.

You.

And so I named you "Strachkvas—Dreadful Feast!"

Father was quite emotional at this point.

He stood, then paced before the fireplace. His dog Mazel looked at him in alarm, and I was shaken myself.

"So do you see? Do you understand I need a way out? I have given myself to Christianity, to a religion that says I can be forgiven! That can open a door to salvation! That is what I need, because it can also send me to hell!

"You, Kristián! If God can forgive me, in this Jesus religion, you must make it happen for me!"

I was witness to the most powerful ruler I have known, now nearly begging his 12-year-old son, still mostly a child, to deliver him from God's punishment for his crime.

I had an eerie feeling about this man-killer before me. My father, demanding I make it all right for him. He was in such a state that I feared for my safety. I was unsure of the law of my faith. What if I told him there was no salvation for those such as he?

But in my agitation, as my priest tutor taught me, I closed my eyes and whispered a prayer, a Psalm:

"I love the Lord, because he hath heard my voice and my supplications.

Because he hath inclined his ear unto me, therefore will I call upon him as long as I live."

I breathed deeply, and as I relaxed, I felt the refuge of God's promise, His love.

I repeated the prayer and sought a moment of peaceful meditation, perhaps louder than a whisper.

"I love the Lord, because he hath heard my voice and my supplications.

Because he hath inclined his ear unto me, therefore will I call upon him as long as I live."

And Father, in the manner he learned as a child from those he loved—Václav and Ludmila—Father joined me.

"I love the Lord, because he doth
    my voice and prayer hear.
And in my days will call, because
    he bowed to me his ear."

I fell silent as my father continued, his childhood memory giving him hope in his soul's strife.

The duke dropped to his knees, and as they taught him as a young boy, placed his hands together and bowed over them.

"The pangs of death on every side
    about beset me round;
the pains of hell got hold of me,

distress and grief I found.
Upon Jehovah's Name therefore
I called, and I did say,
deliver thou my soul, o Lord,
I to Thee humbly pray."

He was the most pitiable of dukes, tortured and tormented by his own deeds.

I stood and left him there that night with his little dog by his side as he strained every tendon and muscle to force his wishes up to God, to where he might hope to find rest at last.

***

Morning again awakened me and the serving woman again brought breakfast to my chamber.

She set the tray upon the pallet and looked at me with tired eyes that spoke of interrupted sleep the night before.

She told me the duke had called all the household to pray with him. "We were all awakened, and he gathered us in the hall. He had us all kneel and led us in prayer.

"We prayed deep into the night, past the setting of the moon, nearly until dawn. We prayed silently on the themes he called, such as that our land would always be fruitful, that we would have peace, and our armies would be victorious when we could not have peace. And he had us all pray for his soul."

I watched the woman, now well past her youth, and knew she wanted to speak. When I became a priest, I would listen to the confessed sins of people, of their hopes and worries. Of their crimes. This serving woman had something on her mind.

She said, "I was in the house of Boleslav during that feast. I saw your uncle the night before he died." Her eyes showed a stress within her. She looked me over and continued, "I was a young woman when you were born. I attended your mother in birth. I was bathing you when your father came to visit your mother the next morning. And I heard the awful name he called you."

There was a moment of silence, and I feared she would call me by that name. I did not know what I would do if she did. I gave a silent prayer that she would not.

"I know what happened, Kristián." The woman closed her eyes for a moment, perhaps in a silent prayer. "And I know too that the duke has mercy within him.

"I should say no more." And she left my chamber.

***

Tira led me again to my father's company. The duke too looked tired, yet there was a fire in him making him restless. He stood before the fire, his hand on his breast, and turned to me as I entered.

"Son, I will tell the rest of my story to you now. Then in the morning, you must leave to begin your life's work."

Father was lit with an inner passion, animated. He sat in his great chair, and his dog stood attentively at his foot. He leaned forward as he spoke.

CHAPTER 9
Prosinec—A Time of Pleading

Hněvsa's men killed most of Václav's party. Some were allowed to escape, whether by Christian members of his household or through common mercy, which all people—pagans, Jews, unbelievers, Muslims, Christians—all share.

Ludmila's servant Mstena, who Václav had inherited, was killed. When he heard of Václav's murder, he flew into a desperate rage, the frail man. He was older now. He fought to avenge his mistress Ludmila and his lord the duke, and indeed sorely wounded two of his attackers before they overcame him.

Podiven escaped into the woods, eventually to Germany, the land of the Franks. No one here saw him for more than a year.

Tuza and his troop of armed men rode to Prague and into the palace of Václav. They laid down all before them and royal chambers ran slick with blood. Most who survived saw no alternative but to swear to Boleslav, their new hereditary duke.

Tuza himself hurried to the quarters of Podiven's wife, Agata. She was gone.

The Danish guards left by Václav in Prague had learned of the plot to kill the duke, and they removed Agata and Václav's young son to hide in the stronghold of Budeč, where Václav had spent his youth studying, learning, praying. All of that training, the wisdom and piety in the saintly man was extinguished.

Veshtak had reminded Tuza that Václav's heir would one day rule, if he survived. Tuza and his men slept for a night at the sacked Prague castle, then gathered a larger force and rode to Budeč.

When they arrived, the Christian Danish guards, greatly outnumbered, called for a parley. Under white flags, their leaders met Tuza. He promised them safe passage with all civilians to the Frankish lands. They returned to their stronghold and prepared to evacuate.

But Tuza was faithless. As the Danish guards left the walls, they were overwhelmed and taken captive, led to a pit. Tuza had them beheaded, and their armor was stolen off their bodies.

Agata, Podiven's wife and the mother of Václav's child, was found hiding in a closet and nursing the toddler.

When she saw Tuza at the door with bared blade, she knew what was happening, and begged him to spare the child. When she stood in his way, wearing her royal temple rings, he slew her with one stroke and had her body dumped in the pit with the Danes.

Then he carried the child to the river.

Tuza later told me the three-year-old child was shocked and afraid, stunned into silence. He did not even scream, but stood in an ultimate fear, stamping and trembling, steadying his feet. Tuza showed nothing of humanity, and brought his bloody sword down through the tender head of my brother's child, my nephew, then tossed the small warm body into the cold waters where it was carried away, the last of Václav's blood mixing with the stream. Maybe sanctifying it?

Dragomira, Mother, learned of the success of her long-prepared plans and was mortified it had actually happened. She was so upset she fled, fearing friends of mine would do her murder. She was right. They would have killed her.

She escaped back to the land of the Croats, where she had lived in her earlier exile and still had friends. She soon became Christian herself and never returned to our lands.

***

My followers persecuted Christians of Prague and burned their churches. Yet even Veshtak's followers feared to destroy St. George's

Basilica where Ludmila rests, and the church my brother built, dedicated to Svatý Vít.

Priests were killed or driven to the Frankish lands or to the East.

Tuza and his men tolerated no dissent, and through their arms, confirmed my rule.

Veshtak and the followers of Svantovít strutted the streets. The remaining Christians hid their ways.

These men ruled harshly. They brought back pagan customs of taking many women, some unwilling, and sacrificing to Svantovít and other pagan gods. The leaders of Tuza's bands took estates of nobles who remained loyal to their fallen Christian duke and displaced them, sometimes keeping their wives, and their daughters too, if they were old enough for their satisfaction.

I was named duke and was feasted and praised with pagan revelry.

In weeks to come I moved into the duke's palace in Prague. They crowned me in ceremony. I sat on the stone throne and was shown the peasant work shoes of Přemysl. I was invested, and I spoke to the people, assuring them I would be strong against their enemies, and I would respect the different religions.

Veshtak did not like that.

But my mind was unsettled.

I remembered Václav's Christian teaching by Grandmother Ludmila, who many Christians regard as a saint. Conscience tormented me, and I spent a cold and worried winter.

Tira, Tuza's gentler brother, became my confidant and friend. I had no wish to see Hněvsa again. My wife moved into the castle with me, not sure of how she should behave at first, being a sensitive woman— who knew, of course, how I came to power, and who did not approve of murder. Perhaps she believed someone might kill me next, along with her. And why not?

I brought Tira to live with me in the palace as my page, to help guard me. He and his brother had become more distant from each other. Tuza, more grasping, perhaps now considered himself a lord, as he had long desired.

I fell into a habit of drunkenness to escape my conscience, and I let my duties languish.

Tuza and some of his men rode to the home of a wealthy Christian farmer. He owned fields near Hněvsa's castle where you were born, and Tuza demanded his home and lands. When he resisted, he killed the man and his sons, one only a child, and violated his woman and daughter before driving them from the estate. Tira found them homeless in the streets of Prague and brought them to me.

I was not corrupted enough to deny them compassion and shelter until they could find another home. The mother from that farm still lives near this castle. His daughter was an assistant to my wife's midwives and serves in my house now. She brought you food this morning.

Across the land, the remaining Christian priests hid in secret camps in the woods, living in monastic simplicity and making no show of religion.

Whenever something is forced upon a people they always react against it. My grandparents Ludmila and Bořivoj learned this when they tried to force our people to accept Christianity in one instant. Now that the old religion was reasserted with the sword, there was resistance, largely because of the examples of holy goodness Václav and Ludmila had set.

They secretly venerated Václav as a holy man, the rightful duke who stood for the goodness of Czechs, and who should lead them to holy righteousness, even in death. By allowing Veshtak's harshness, my rule did not compare well with that of my gentle brother. This contrast generated Christian converts.

Ludmila, our martyred grandmother, was also quietly praised as the person who brought Christian light to our people. Our land's wealth of harvests still proves her success at every feast, both pagan and Christian.

You, Kristián, were only an infant, and your brother, young Boleslav, was but a lad.

At first, the servants and guards we brought into the castle were anxious. They expected conflict and battle from the townspeople, but Veshtak, Tuza and their men cowed the citizens. Servants from Hrad Boleslav quickly became familiar with life in Prague Castle and the pleasures and commerce of the city.

Among all the murderous activities in the weeks and months following Václav's death, those events shook the people who were not involved or who did not benefit directly.

Some shared their concerns with Dušan.

Some found secret Christian brothers who had kept and duplicated the original texts of Methodius and Cyril. They took counsel with them and heard words of Jesus, and the Psalms, which you know better than I:

"I prayed to the Lord, and he answered me;
    he freed me from all my fears.
The oppressed look to him and are glad;
    they will never be disappointed.
The helpless call to him, and he answers;
    he saves them from all their troubles.
His angel guards those who honor the Lord
    and rescues them from danger."

And the words of Jesus:

"Blessed are those who mourn,
For they shall be comforted.
Blessed are the meek,
For they shall inherit the earth.
Blessed are those who hunger and thirst for righteousness,
For they shall be filled.
Blessed are the merciful,
For they shall obtain mercy.
Blessed are the pure in heart,
For they shall see God.
Blessed are the peacemakers,
For they shall be called sons of God.

Blessed are those who are persecuted for righteousness' sake,

For theirs is the kingdom of heaven."

Now, other faiths may have similar scriptures, I don't know. But those words have power and reassurance in our wicked world. It is the message everyone wants!

And there is an invitation in them that leads people to the Christian religion.

Unlike the counsel of whatever pagan priest you may meet, and some of them are good and wholesome, like Dušan, these words are written and consistent, if not always emphasized by all priests. They speak to basic human truth, of desire for a just god, for comfort and mercy.

Christianity is appealing for many reasons. One part is the magical story of the virgin birth, and that the sacrifice of Jesus, the human son of God, can atone for everyone's sins. The bloody death and the resurrection of a dead person is macabre enough for those who love that sort of tale. And the underlying order of the story is better than the confusion of Svantovít, Veles, Morana of our old religion, or the venal lasciviousness of the Roman gods or those of the Northmen. The Christian Faith is built upon the ancient and time-tested historic myths of the Jews.

But its chief appeal is Jesus's message of love and forgiveness.

***

Dušan kept to his furnaces and pits of smoke, fire, hammers, and loyal workers. He also had pagan followers, who were no friends of Veshtak.

Myself, I returned to pagan ways, or at least their venal lusts. I sinned. I murdered. I drank to excess. Of the seven deadly sins I practiced them all, and was burdened by them.

But the new religion says I can be forgiven. Kristián, is this true, even of me? Would Jesus allow it? But then I sought relief and comfort with the old ways.

I took obeisance from citizens and landowners in the region and accepted their gifts of silver and honey. They gave promises of cattle, grain and horses, of oaths sworn to my service, and fine trinkets for my body and for my wife's pleasure.

Yet my heart was clouded.

I kept to myself in the palace at Prague, while Tuza and Hněvsa stormed through the frozen land, pillaging churches and Christian farms too weak to oppose them. Some Christians banded together and defended themselves well, and it became necessary to make an armed truce with them.

We heard whispers of miracles at the site of Václav's murder. They could not wash his blood from the paving stones, and lights would flash and glow where his body was buried. It became a site of pilgrimage for believers, and some spoke against my rule.

I don't blame them.

Finally, I had the body of my brother—who I had martyred!—reassembled and brought to Prague. He is interred in the church he had built to the Sicilian martyr Saint Vitus, Svatý Vít, whose name is so like that of Svantovít.

I was restless at night and my sleep was troubled. I often dreamed and saw the face of my brother, sometimes with a mark of blood on his forehead from the stroke of my blade.

Oh, my heart was not well. I was sore in spirit. I looked to my friendly priest and counselor of the old religion. Yet even his gentle words gave me no peace.

***

In early spring and into the summer I started roving on walks, alone at night.

My path trailed into the woods, to fields guarded by shepherds and their dogs, or just birds of the night. I might see a fox or hedgehog, or perhaps a ranging wolf.

On one such walk I stepped from the forest into a field of low grass and bright stars. A nightjar flew up in my face and hovered, looking me over, as if to challenge my right in his field. When he left, the stars spread like a blanket of glimmer over me. I heard the distant, eerie rumbling of Kamil's fujara flute.

I hadn't realized I was so close to Dušan's realm. I walked toward the sound.

When I was near the charcoalliery I paused. The entire area was swathed in dense fog mixed with smokes from cooking wood, and dimly lit with greenish and bluish glows from the pits.

My vision was very limited as I walked slowly into that nether world of smoke and sound. Though I was awake, the blend of resonant throbbing of the flute and the mist and cloud created an unreal, spectral world.

Dušan was speaking with Bratumil, the worker with the eyebrow across his forehead. I could not make out words, but heard his voice, deep within the music from Kamil's fujara.

I knew Bratumil was a Christian, taught by Podiven, and that Dušan still spoke for the old gods.

Usually, Dušan listened and gave counsel in his gentle way to those citizens of my realm who sought him. Now it looked as if he was taking counsel from his former slave.

I turned away. Unseen by either, I walked from the smoky vale and into the woods again.

***

I've always been told there is magic in the forest, and I still believe it.

My steps followed paths unfamiliar to me, and I wandered far in the wood. The very trees—perhaps their good spirits—seemed to whisper at me, to chide me for a murderer, a cursed usurper and fratricide.

Other spirit whispers told me, "All is well. You succeeded and became duke!" The whispers of snakes!

The trail I followed branched off to smaller trails, and on I wandered into the night.

The darkness was deep. The silence gave me no rest from my thoughts.

There were nymphs among the trees, according to the old tales. There were ogres there, too. I felt myself the most depraved ogre of them all.

The faint path I tread divided into two; one led up a hill, the other trended down to moister regions. I chose the lower.

Creatures rustled in the dark.

My eyes had become night-wise, and I felt them bulge like great orbs. A faint halo of blueish glow formed about my vision.

I peered ahead. Little starlight penetrated below the forest canopy.

I used my sword as a blind man uses his cane. I bumped against trunks of trees, and yet still further I journeyed, searching this blackness for I know now what, this enchanted region of sightlessness and small sounds.

Ahead, I fancied I saw a dim light. I stepped toward it, and it remained aglow.

There are tales of fairy lights in the deep forest where dryads gather, or a spirit of light might stand alone, guarding its tree or grove.

I sought something, something. A salvation I could not name.

Slowly my steps brought me to an opening in the woods, still dark, yet I saw a sparkle of light in the deep.

There was no animate thing near me, no night squirrel, no wild boar, no hart, no bird. But the dim light drew me onward.

I stopped and leaned against the bole of a mighty oak and rubbed my eyes. I looked into shadow where the sparkle lived, and could make out something—a form, a woman. The spirit of the tree?

Memory took me back to the night when the oracle tried to kill Dušan, the same night Grandmother was killed—by Mother's friends! The oracle had a carnelian pendant, and hers was a swaying figure, like the pulsating dim shape before me.

The blue faux lights encircling my eyes were as bright as the twinkling wood-nymph form. It seemed to change and re-form itself, now into an image of bare-breasted Saskia beckoning me to nurse from her body, my gentle first friend, who I had sent from our land so my mother could not use even her as a force against me.

I walked toward the spots of light and they sprang apart, dissipating into the fireflies or glow-worms they were, to hide under leaves and brush and debris at the bottom of the wet depression I stepped into.

My foot sank into mud, which for a thousand years the forest kept soft with its seep, ancient home of worms, salamanders, snakes, forest bugs—the thoughtless creatures whose domain I had entered. I was one of them now.

I felt the earth's moisture creep into my boot, as if my body was to take root, and I to change into a tree, and become one with the forest.

After a moment, I pulled my foot from the sucking bog and sat heavily on the ground. I was lost in the dark wood, muddy, forlorn.

I wept.

I was duke, lord of the land. All must bow before me, yet there I sat, wet and friendless here in this desert forest, becoming hungry, yet not feeling it, not caring. Hating myself for the crime I had committed.

I felt vile.

I was mortified at my life. Boleslav! "Greater Glory!"

I lay back on leaves, exhaling sobs. Then I noticed I could see branches above in the darkness. Their shadows seemed to move. How could this be?

I sat up, turned my head and saw a shape, a hooded and caped person holding a lamp suspended from a rod. Another hooded figure was behind.

The light was dim, an oil lamp enclosed in pierced hide. Its yellowish glow cast mild, moving shadows about the two forms.

They approached me, unafraid.

The shaded faces looked down on where I laid.

In a garbled speech one said, "Who." More a command than a question.

"Murderer," I said.

The one hood bent to the other and whispered. Then they nodded. They seemed not afraid of me or my sword "Kingmaker" as I lay in despair in the dark.

"Come," said the one not holding the lamp.

This seemed more a plan of action than just lying in mud, hoping for an apparition of fireflies.

As I stood, I saw these two were small, old women. Gray hair snaked from the hood of one with the lamp. The other beckoned with a small shriveled hand, and I followed.

We walked into the clearing, which I slowly realized was the same glade where I was lost the day of the hunt. We passed through the center and I saw again the panel of woven twigs, and now in its center were woven crane feathers glowing white in the night.

Not far past the open glade, we picked up a trail a bit more used than the one that led me here, still not well-defined. It could have been a deer track.

The trail turned a bit to the right and led further into deep woods. At the same point an even fainter trail led beside a linden tree, and on this trail they led me.

We passed a massive boulder covered in moss and lichen, and as the woman silently led me in her bubble of faint light, we entered a tunnel of woven branches of willow and ash, its entrance invisible until you were right upon it.

A white hand from the cloak of the crone opened a gate of vines, and we entered a yard twelve paces wide, open to the sky, and lit by three oil lamps. Three dogs watched us as we entered, silent yet wary. To one side was a woven fence holding a few goats.

I saw a third woman tending an earthen pot over a fire and chanting some words, perhaps reciting an herbarium of lore, timing her infusion as Dušan times his furnaces. When she saw me—noticed my sword— she started in alarm, until the lamp-bearer whispered to her.

The woman behind me told me to sit on a stool made of a tree stump. She spoke with the others and brought me a bowl of soup.

I admit I was hungry in my muddy despair, and I brought the clay bowl to my lips. It smelled of roots, and mint, and garlic. She gave me cheese and bread of oats and millet, and asked to hear my story.

I was not comfortable there, but was exhausted in body and mind.

I told her my tale, and as I did, I revealed my story to myself with more understanding than I ever had before.

Mother had raised me to use as her tool to regain the power she loved when she was the duke's wife. When he died and Ludmila took my brother to raise to become ruler, Dragomira trained me to do her bidding, to grow into the one person who could return her to power as the strong mother of a compliant ruler. She brought Veshtak, Tunna and his sons, and the father of Hněvsa into her circle. They led me to believe it was my duty, my fate to become duke, that it was not wrong to supplant my brother by whatever means needed. To my everlasting infamy and damnation!

I wept.

The three sisters gathered and spoke among themselves.

I don't know they had any powers I would term magical, yet they did have totems, charms and fetishes about the yard. Talismans of bits of cloth, and feathers, of tufts of wool tied to branches about the trail: the tail of a horse, the tooth of a wolf, a claw of a bear. Also dried flowers and herbs. Some totems were woven into patterns of basketry. I recognized these items as being of a kind with the one I found the day when I was separated from my hunting companions. The small trellis-works were elaborated with items of stone or herb, and perhaps told a story, or a prayer, or cast a spell.

The third woman continued to stir the soup or whatever it was simmering in an earthen pot over the fire. She tasted it.

One dog laid back on its side and nursed five puppies. Life goes on. The other curs watched me.

I noticed a wooden door at the hill's base, which seemed to lead into the wall of rock that defined part of the yard. They must sleep in the cave, but this night they were up late. In fact, it was nearly morning.

The cook ladled some of her brew into the bowl I had drunk the wholesome soup from. The woman who led me here brought it to me.

She placed some bits of herb in the bowl, and the hot liquid began steeping. She sprinkled some white blossoms of holy linden onto the brew's surface.

The woman to whom I had told my tale said, "Purge."

I did not dispute her, but a purge of my soul was what I needed— not some bowel-cleansing herb broth.

My heart was docile, and I drank the liquid. I grew drowsy and laid on the forest floor on a blanket of fleece.

I slept a deep and dreamless sleep.

At first.

Then visions came.

I saw three figures take shape, the pagan priestesses of ancient lore, daughters of Krok: Kazi with knowledge of herbs and with the gift of healing, Teta the religious priestess who spoke with the gods, and wise Libuše of prophesies. The three spoke in one voice and said, "The old ways are passing. You are leader of our people now."

Libuše, the sister of sight who had married Přemysl the Plowman said, "Duke Boleslav, there are many ages ahead for the people of Czech. They will struggle against enemies and sometimes be subdued. They will nearly lose that which makes us unique, even our language, but they will find it again, and flourish as a sovereign people honored among nations. Your actions as duke will lead them to this future."

"The old ways are passing," said Teta, who spoke with the gods. "The new age is upon us. Use your power and your judgement, won by trial and tragedy. Guide them with good sense to their spiritual home."

Kazi, the healer, told me, "Guide them with strength. Use your grandmother's new crops to make them strong. You are duke. Lead your people into the world ahead. The old ways are passing."

Then the three priestesses, my family from ancient pagan days of old, themselves passed into mist among the trees.

I dreamed I was in the chapel of the castle of Tetín. Grandmother Ludmila drifted into my sight, her prayer scarf loosely wrapped about her neck, and light shining around her head. She looked at me with an inquiring gaze and whispered to me, "Grandson, where is Václav? Is he at prayer?" She turned to look for him, chanting a psalm, and left me. I tried to follow her, but my legs were leaden. I called to her, but she did not slow, and walked away to kneel at a distant altar where candles burned.

I turned around and looked down from a height as if from eyes of Svantovít's eagle upon the city of Prague. It was deserted now, without color or sound. It was as if all people had been drawn away, leaving empty streets, empty shops, empty houses. All was empty.

In my dream I ran through the town and past the slave market, past the Jewish quarter to the river in misty twilight. The Vltava was silent and still. A cloudy shroud hung over it. No fishermen worked its waters.

I watched the river flow, and on its dark surface, the body of a young child drifted by me. As it passed, he turned his face to me and gave me a wondering stare, then turned away and drifted into darkness.

Mother's face appeared, Dragomira, grinning in triumph, showing sharpened teeth, her eyes dark. Veshtak, and Tunna, Gomon, and Tuza joined her. Tira hung back, but Hněvsa came into the group, and all smiled. Mother said, "Boleslav! Great Glory!" Veshtak said, "Duke Boleslav! Glory to Svantovít!" The others cheered, but Tira looked at me with a solemn face. He stepped back, back, away into shadow.

I heard the words, "Brother. Let us not spill blood of our family this night," and when I turned to the voice, I saw the dismembered body of Václav lying on Hněvsa's pavement, a mark from my sword on his forehead, Tuza and Hněvsa smiling and cheering each other at the abomination.

My chest burned where I had wiped Václav's blood over my heart. I clawed at the spot. I felt as if blood filled my eyes, and I ran away into deep woods where Svantovít and Veles and yes, Morana might give me some solace. The Green Eternal Hunter and his dog passed by. They stopped, and both stood still, watching as I fled.

Svantovít was a warrior god and he would understand why I had to do the deed. He would cheer me and give me peace about killing Václav, the weak leader who would rather pray than conquer, rather forgive than punish. Swords are better than books!

I ran to the crossroads, where a statue of Svantovít had looked down on all travelers through these groves on this earth. But his statue was not there.

Instead, there stood an image of the Christian saint, mother of Jesus, Svatá Mary. Her face was kind, and smiled at me, forgiving. And as I watched, the statue became a goddess' image of Velká Matka Země, "Great Mother Earth," still smiling in conditionless love.

This was not what I needed, this goddess of kindness, of fertility, weaving and harvest, of gentle words and love. I did not need love! I wanted justification!

A priestess of Matka Země stepped from behind the statue of her goddess. She was tall and fair, young-looking, and appeared as fertile as her goddess's promise.

There was no god of war to justify my act. Only this woman. In my frustration, I would act upon her!

My hands found the belt on her cape. She did not cry, nor smile, nor resist.

I struck her with my open hand—a great sin to strike the priestess— and she did not speak.

Did I hate even the very earth?

I threw her to the ground, determined to perform an even greater transgression than killing my Christian brother—my brother! Only in the old religion would this be worse!

I opened my clothes and drove into the priestess, and she did not react.

I thrust and thrust, a base urge, sending my seed into her.

And… she changed.

The priestess of Matka Země became less defined, more of earth, until finally there was no woman, just myself pitching and driving into earth's moist clay itself, then slowing, and not harshly, but more gently, more loving, and I wept at my sins.

I became one with the earth. I felt myself renewing and awakening, with creatures of the forest about me. Birds, animals, ferns, trees. I could feel them, heard their sounds, feel their warm breath on my skin, and reached to touch and embrace them all. I stroked feathers, and touched the fur of animals, and felt the grateful tongue of a beast on my hand.

I came to myself and awoke to broad noon in the dim trackless forest, and I was alone—except for the beast.

A large furry animal was standing over me, my hands deep in its fur. I felt again its tongue on my hand, and I started awake. This was no dream!

I sat up and scrambled back with a feeling of danger, of being attacked by this animal, this bear, this wolf! Or... dog.

Yes, this was a dog. And I knew his name: Král.

Král sat back and watched me, alert but tail wagging, as I came to my sense in the dappled dark of the forest floor.

Král! Dušan must be near.

I looked about me in the full light of noon beneath the forest canopy and saw no one in the shadows amid the tree boles.

A glory of sunbeams shafted down.

When I came fully to myself, I staggered to my feet and looked about. Král waited, watching me. My clothes were creased and muddied, my sword was nearby on the ground.

I realized the three old hermit sisters had fed me a draft that drew me out of myself. The sisters had heard my tale and used their herbal skills to open a way for me.

They had carried me here and laid me in the forest, to let me travel on my mind's path, as I sought my purpose. The dream of Grandmother, and of Mother and of Václav, and then the dryad priestess. It was indeed a purge of my soul.

But to what end?

"Let's go, boy," I said to the dog, and he turned and walked through the trees, directly to his master. I followed, a bit wobbly.

I saw Dušan in the distance, bending to gather plants or seeds, roots, spores, nuts, whatever he needed for his priestly duties. He was dressed in a brown robe, with a few pouches slung from his shoulders. A cavern's entrance opened behind him.

The sight of the robed figure in columns of sunbeams looked natural, as if he belonged here in the boreal world of oaks and linden, club moss and mushroom.

I stopped and watched him as Král went to his side. Dušan looked up, and his gaze found me. He waved his hand, and after a moment, bent again to his task. He had his labor.

And I had mine.

I was not lost now. I had always known where I was, more or less, in the trackless woods. I walked to the shore of the Vltava River that flows through Prague. It was nearby, and I followed the river trail up to where it led north and west, back into the forest. In the dimness of a darkening twilight I came to where a four-headed stone figure of Svantovít stood at the ancient crossroads.

It was not safe for a lone traveler in the woods, daytime or night. Even the duke.

Or rather, as lately proven, perhaps especially the duke.

I paused at the pagan figure. It had been thrown down in Václav's time. Someone had restored it to its place, a bit chipped from its fall, yet still commanding.

Someone had placed food at its feet; a pile of wheat, some turnips, cabbages, apples. A few apples made my afternoon meal. I turned my face to the path to Prague and stepped forth, keeping my hand on my sword. I was aware trees and shrubs to the sides of the trail could hide brigands or assassins.

Ahead of me on the trail, I heard the sound of hoofs. I stepped into the shadow of a maple and watched as three horsemen passed, one of them my page Tira.

"Hail!" I called, and the party stopped.

For an instant I feared I had called to men who would kill a duke, to open a door of power to their masters.

But Tira was faithful. He told a horseman to dismount, and I took his ride and returned with him to the palace.

CHAPTER 10
Duben—In the Oak Grove

My rule as duke was based on a heinous crime. I supported worship of gods in what I was growing to believe was a backward religion. Its customs and doctrines could follow whims of whatever priest could gain power over a congregation. Veshtak was the worst demonstration of that; Dušan was not.

Dušan was not.

The past is past. Deeds are unchangeable. What has happened will remain forever unalterable. But perhaps it is possible to make amends—some, at least.

I resolved to seek Dušan once again, to share my thoughts with my friend, the gentle priest of Svantovít. I touched the amulet he gave me those years ago.

***

Days grew short. Skies were more cloudy than clear. Early snows had blown across the land.

Harvest feasting was done; the customs of Yule were approaching. They minded me of the popular story of Václav and his page giving wood to the peasant, then blessing his hovel. He blessed the evergreen bough with his words, with holy wafers he himself had formed, baked, and sanctified.

On a cold, cloudless day, I cloaked myself in wool. With my friend and page Tira, I set out to the charcoal pits and a meeting with Dušan.

As we drew near, I heard the music of flutes, Kamil's flute in high pitch, with a deep guttural bass, all in a slow tune, nearly a dirge, and another flute blending a slow and hopeful tune atop of it.

I followed Tira across a field of frozen morning dew, crystal gems of ice sparkling in sunlight, and saw smoke rising from the ironworks. I heard hammering from the forge, beating the rhythms of workers, flutes playing in time with heartbeat-like throbs of hammers forming our tools from the earth.

The flute music grew louder as we approached Kamil and Dušan. His dog Král, older now, leapt to greet me.

The priest took the flute from his lips, and he turned the glow of his remarkable personality to me.

He said quietly, "Boleslav. Have you discovered your path?"

My path.

The paths of my days were unwholesome and brought me agony.

Yet each day begins anew.

Dušan knew this, and beyond telling this hopeful truth, he demonstrated it. He came to me and opened his arms in greeting. The light of the new day shone around him, beams of sunlight from the sky.

About his neck hung the chain holding his green comet-stone.

And it was set in a shining silver cross.

***

Dušan and I spent the day talking.

Well, I talked.

Tira and Kamil spent their time with conversations, perhaps much like our own.

I felt there was much to discuss. Dušan convinced me there was not.

I asked how he could exchange Svantovít and Veles's laws for the Church's laws, and he revealed he had not changed.

"There is much that is good in the old ways," he told me. "Matka Země's fruitfulness, Veles's goodness of the harvest, our ways of kindness to others. These are not so different from words of Jesus and his disciples."

His earlier knowledge of writing was of pagan runes, not letters of Latin and Greek. In future days he made some efforts to learn the translations the Holy Brothers had created, but his reading was limited. He was older now, and learned to read only the Psalms and the Gospels Methodius and Cyril had translated. These were enough. He found goodness and meaning in those.

Jesus, in his teachings, said there was no other way than through him. Dušan interpreted that to mean the way was through his message. That was not so different from the best of what the old gods had revealed to him in shapes of clouds, the forms of growing trees and ferns, the sound of birds and beasts, the laughter of children, and in patterns of stars and waters. He said, "All reveal the wonder of the gods—of God. They help us find harmony and how people should live. To help them love each other."

That is what the message is. Love. All else is simply a means to achieve that goal.

What all people want!

"But what about images of the gods?" I asked.

He said, "Replace them with images of Holy Mother Mary, and of Jesus and the saints. The good messages they bear are the same."

I thought of the vein of gold within the crystal amulet he had given me, which I still wear about my neck. See it here?

I knew there were Christians—as well as followers of the old religion—who did not believe in a simple message of love. They were adamant in following minutiae of behavior, of praying at prescribed times, specific offerings on holy days, Holy Communion, live sacrifices. Some involved shaming and denouncing those who did not follow ways approved by the priest, demands by the Church to decry particular practices. "All of that is politics," said Dušan. "See the basic needs men seek, and women, too. A way to live together in love. I have always guided my people to that."

Yet politics is often not abstract. The Franks continue to press us, demanding tribute, forcing their priests on us who demand obedience to exacting laws favoring their kings.

Many had died resisting that change.

"Remove the old idols, build churches," said Dušan. "The press of new ways cannot be denied, so accept what you must, and keep what you know you should.

"Do not defend old ways. Their time is past. Find goodness in the new religion. There is much goodness there!"

And so Dušan led his pagan followers—and me—to the message of Christ.

***

I will never be as pious and holy as Václav was, but I work to our country's benefit. I now help spread the goodness of his works, stabilizing justice, and supporting new agriculture.

My men and I were away touring the land and arranging for a system of defense when a deadly ghost visited Prague. Many believe those who die and are not burned or decapitated can rise from their graves and walk the land. This ghost was no vampire, but a devoted living servant.

Podiven returned, the loyal page of my dead brother. His wife and beloved adopted son—the blood son of Václav and my own nephew— were killed during the wild purge of Christians after Václav's murder.

Tuza had led the men who flushed Václav's people from the castle in Prague, and then the horror in Budeč. Podiven had escaped from Hněvsa's castle and was still travelling through the forest to home when Tuza killed Agata, and taken the poor prince child to the river, where he clove his small head and cast him into the water.

In just two days Podiven had lost his master, his station, his wife, his beloved stepson… everything he cared about in his world.

He wandered away to the Frankish kingdom, where he met other refugees. Podiven wanted revenge, but the others were dispirited and chose to stay with the Germans and learn their ways.

After a year, Podiven put vengeance above reason and took retribution on his duke's killers. He returned alone to the Prague iron works where he met with Bratumil, his fellow prisoner from the erased village of Good Home. He greeted the master bladesmith of the Prague armory as his friend. One man was a slave who became a craftsman and a leader of workers. The other had been the duke's manservant and lived in the palace, but had lost everything.

Podiven inquired about Václav's killers. Bratumil told him Tira had turned away from the others and become my Christian ally. As for the others, Hněvsa, my childhood friend of old, had met a horrible death.

Hněvsa inherited his father's wealth and lived in a hamlet with many houses, workers, and slaves.

His father had built a strong foundation flock of sheep and traded meat, fleece and wool for everything else he needed. He bred strong shepherd dogs for herding and protection of his flock. As a child, Hněvsa grew up in the wealth of his father's home and with the attention of slaves.

He had been my friend and training partner. Podiven knew him, too.

But Hněvsa grew up too pampered, a child of privilege. He expected a life of ease, for all to bend to his will, and did little work despite his father's commands. He knew he could eat from his father's success and would have good clothes, a horse, concubines, whatever he wanted. And he was cruel when dealing with animals and slaves.

When his father became older, he railed at Hněvsa about his laziness, while the old man continued to work his flocks with his dogs, even when he became aged and infirm.

Hněvsa took to the hunt to escape his father's criticism. He spent weeks in the forest with his fellows, wasting his life.

When the time came for me to... ah, become duke, the week of your birth feast, he joined in the tragic sin I bear. He helped me kill my brother.

When his father finally died, Hněvsa continued his irresponsible ways. His flocks diminished, he mistreated and starved his dogs, and some even became feral. His workers and slaves were not happy. Their lives degraded, and many ran away.

Hněvsa traded away his wealth to continue his unrestrained life of pleasure. He continued his hunting, and many thought their lives would be better if he never returned from the chase.

One night at home he complained of pain in his back, and of trouble moving his feet. His behavior grew erratic, and he slept for a whole day at a time, or would stay up for days and nights without sleep.

Hněvsa began to refuse food and drink, and finally his behavior was so extreme he lashed out at his servants, even his friends. He spoke loudly, without words, and was horribly agitated. He crawled on the ground; he yelled and barked like a dog. No one could stand his company, and they locked him in his house, as he senselessly raged. After another day he became comatose, and then he died.

When his men entered his house again, they saw Hněvsa had destroyed every precious thing his father had left him, everything of value.

They burned him in his house, and he and all his father had made were destroyed.

One of his Christian workers told me he was sure it was God's judgement on him for Václav's murder. And some of his men spoke of an event that had happened two months earlier, in the warm month of small red worms.

Hněvsa was hunting in the deep forest to the east. The men who were with him had outpaced him, and he slowed to determine which path they had taken. When the men returned to find him, they saw he had encountered a dog acting strangely. This was a dog from his farm, one who his abuse had driven away to the forest. He was not fearful of Hněvsa now.

The dog had apparently spooked Hněvsa's mount, which threw him from his saddle.

Hněvsa faced the feral dog. It was unsteady on its feet, enraged, and made rough and gurgling growls, with saliva dripping from its muzzle. Hněvsa held his arm where the animal had apparently bitten him.

The companions shot the dog with arrows, and it ran away into the brush to die, choking and howling in an unholy sound.

From their tale, many thought the gods were punishing him, that he was becoming an animal himself, perhaps a beast like the dog who bit him.

Perhaps it was God's punishment on the killer of Podiven's master. Kristián, if this could happen to him, God's punishment on me could be worse!

Bratumil knew where Tuza, the other murderer, lived. He led Podiven to his estate outside my old castle, Hrad Boleslav. Podiven thanked his friend and told Bratumil he should leave the village and return to his home and hearth. This was to be the vengeance of Václav's page alone.

Bratumil had given Podiven a fine blade bearing a curse upon those whose blood it would draw.

With a last embrace, Bratumil said goodbye to his old friend and to the last person who could share his childhood memories of their destroyed home village, where they played together as very young boys. They both silently recalled the terror their families had endured. Yet they also shared a few words of happy memories of living there with their fathers and mothers—all that children really want.

Bratumil returned to his smoky world of ringing iron and to his good future.

Podiven arrived at the home of Tuza, who was relaxing in the sauna house. Podiven called, "Let me in! I am cold!" and entered. Tuza greeted him as if he were a visiting neighbor, "Welcome Friend!"

Podiven revealed who he was, and the page of Václav saw the murderer's terror. Tuza cried out as the avenger of his master satisfied what he saw was his duty.

He struck the murderer many times with his sword and utterly destroyed him.

Tuza's scream raised the alarm and Podiven fled. Once again, he escaped into the forest after a bloody killing.

For a night and a day men and hounds of Tuza chased him before they cornered him, and their dogs brought him to bay. He was lanced like a boar, and his body was hung from the limb of a holy Linden tree.

I came upon him several months later, and his body was still intact. I had him buried beneath the Linden, sacred to the pagans. I see no reason it shouldn't be sacred to the Czechs. God made the tree as surely as he made anything else in the world.

News of Podiven's actions made him a popular hero. Christian followers of Václav sought out the grave and left candles and offerings. I eventually had him exhumed and moved into the graveyard of the Church of Svatý Vít where Václav lays. Podiven attends him in death as he had in life, a loyal page for eternity.

Did Podiven sin in taking his vengeance? I don't know. I don't know what true sin is. Well, yes, I know some things are sins. But is each man to judge? Can anyone put his faith into the words of a priest? His whole faith? Dušan told me there was a bit of a god, now Christ's God, within me. And as with his little metal doll, I am drawn to some ways—not always God's way.

But now I try.

***

I saw a clear path now. I took up my saintly brother's tasks.

I must choose a religion, so I chose to follow the words of Christ! I give myself wholly to it, and seek to find the forgiveness he promises! Restore my soul!

I distanced myself farther from counsels of Veshtak, and drew closer to Erhard, Václav's Christian priest. I found him in a forest community of monks and brought him back to Prague.

At the first of the new year, I decreed all people should welcome back Christians. Churches were reopened, re-sanctified, and new ones created in villages from Budeč to Hrad Boleslav and beyond.

I told my people to put away old gods. To symbolize this, we chose one: the goddess Morana, to represent all the old gods as an example.

In the holy days of Lent all over our lands, straw images of that pagan goddess of death are brought to lakes where her clothes are torn and the effigy set afire. We make no mention now of other things she represented.

Every year Morana's burnt image is drowned in the waters as we are drowning the old beliefs. The act symbolizes the end of winter, but more importantly, it builds community. It lets people join in rejection of the old religion, and on a Christian holiday.

I brought the country forward by destroying every visible vestige of old religions and by combining old rituals with compatible Christian ones when possible. As expected, some people resisted this.

As we again pulled down the images of Svantovít and Veles, they were pulverized and spread as gravel fragments where they once stood. I erected stone markers and shrines along our roads, proclaiming this is the land of Czechs, and is Christian.

Veshtak sensed discomfort in some people. He called a council of his remaining followers and an old, one-eyed pagan priest. They saw their strength waning, eclipsed by my increasing Christian power. The bitter priest from Kourim had found Veshtak and together they plotted once again to murder a Christian duke, to supplant me with some compliant cousin from a sister's distant family.

Once again, word spread for people loyal to the teachings of Veshtak to meet at the holy oak grove, where years earlier Dušan had brought an oracle to see into the dark future, and she had foretold the murder of Grandmother Ludmila. Veshtak directed all to bring a lamb, a measure of grain, a fowl, some kind of sacrifice to strengthen their commitment to his teachings and to follow him in his plotting.

I was here at Hrad Prague, and later heard that about sixty of Veshtak's followers met at a bonfire in the grove held at night, as was usual with Veshtak's meetings. They were men, young and older, all armed.

An idol of Svantovít had stood at the north edge of the clearing. It was pulled down during the reign of my brother. Václav had rededicated the glade to Svatý Vít, and a small shrine built where

Svantovít's four-headed statue had stood. Veshtak removed the Christian shrine immediately when I was crowned duke and had replaced it with another figure of the old god, less elaborate, hastily carved.

As the service got underway, the priests led those gathered to chant a prayer hymn to Svantovít. Each in turn brought his sacrifice to the fire and cast it into the blaze, with a prayer from Veshtak and the one-eyed priest. A basket of wheat, a bound squirming piglet, a measure of oats, a bundle of hides, a lamb, each was ceremoniously thrown on the fire as the worshipers came forward.

The men became aware of others at the glade's edge.

The chanting and drums slowed and stopped. Into the center of the grove strode Dušan in his priestly robes, wearing his cross pendant. He was flanked by his apprentice Kamil and by his large bladesmith Bratumil, of the single eyebrow.

Dušan stepped forward and loudly said, "This is the sacred glade of Saint Vitus, no longer holy to old false gods!" And with those words Bratumil, bearing a great hammer from the forge, walked to the pagan god statue and with a mighty blow knocked it to the ground, and with another broke it in two.

The worshippers gasped, and as one, they moved to the center of the clearing.

Veshtak called to them, "Men of Svantovít and Veles! Clear the glade of these faithless men!" Arms were drawn, and the men advanced.

Kamil raised a horn to his lips and blew a blast. From all around the edge of the glade workers of Dušan stepped into view, visible in the light from the bright fire. They numbered about sixty, each carrying their tools, a hammer or axe. The two forces were well matched—the strong workers, the armed pagans.

Veshtak came near Dušan and called, "Your faith has no power here!" He spoke in a loud voice, "The weak god who was nailed to a tree will not chase Svantovít from his holy grove!"

He walked by the bonfire and drew from his secret pockets small pouches of a substance I later learned were the dry spores of club moss. It makes a good show.

Veshtak threw the small packets into the fire and they popped with bright, instant flashes that sparkled in brilliant white light, nearly blinding all who stood there.

Dušan spoke a word to Kamil, and from a bag on his shoulder he handed a bundle of fine fox furs to his master, who spoke to all the men there:

"This is my offering to the fire in this holy place. I cast it into the fire I dedicate to the Lord God, Who was worshipped by St. Vitus, Svatý Vít!"

Dušan held the bundle of fur above his head. "I give you this gift to the one God as a last sacrifice for your service!" He cast the bundle of valuable furs into the bonfire. A shower of sparks spiraled into the night sky as fibers of fur snapped and spat in the blaze.

"You will not stay here long. You will see the ways of the Lord God are great!"

Dušan walked away and his followers faded from the oak glade.

Veshtak cautiously watched them leave and walked to the great blaze he had built to honor Svantovít and Veles and the old gods. The priest stood with his arms and staff held high to the blaze, a black silhouette against bright flames, then said, "See the power of Svantovít! Those who worship the weak god who was killed on a tree cannot stand before him! They even give a sacrifice to his power!"

And then a miracle occurred.

This was not a miracle such as healing a lame man, nor curing a coughing babe. This was not the miracle of bringing a harvest from a stricken field, or changing sour wine into sweet. This was more akin to a bolt from Svantovít. Or perhaps some greater god.

The priest Dušan had long tended his forges at the edge of Prague, a city which stood astride four great roads of commerce.

He met many pilgrims and traders from far to the ultimate west— Iberia, where emasculated Polish and Czech slaves are sold to Moorish kings, and all land ends at a great sea; and from northern Scandinavia, where mystic lights dance in the sky. He spoke with men from the wilds of Ireland, the edge of the western world, and from the fabled paved city of Rome itself. Dušan had discussed faith and trade with Jews from Kazakhstan, with worshippers of fire from Persia. Late into the night, he and Kamil had spoken with Russians, with Scythians, with Burgundians. And a few men he met were from the very eastern end of earth where there are great civilizations on islands in unknown oceans.

Some of these learned men from Indus and beyond could discuss the very nature of mankind and the universe. They spoke of how men should treat each other in a way that often sounded like words of Jesus.

The needs of men are the same throughout the world.

Traders brought amber from the Baltic, and new ways of smelting silver which we use today, and lore of strange herbs and grains, mysterious cloth spun by worms, secrets of minerals, and even ways to make a new sort of fire.

One skill some of them shared with Dušan was formulation of a compound of charcoal, of which Prague had a ready supply, Sulphur, of which he knew well, and certain crystals found in caves where bats slept. Like the cave I had seen him near that morning after awakening from my dream.

This Sulphur and charcoal mixture seemed magic to those who did not know its formula. But it was simply an example of the wonder of the world God made, and it allowed the display of godlike power.

Veshtak's bonfire, the simple fire of wood which devoured other sacrifices, accepted the bound fox skin package thrown by Dušan. Then that bundle of hides revealed it held a mixture of Sulphur, charcoal and crystals that became the wrath of all gods, of the Almighty God of ancient Jewish scriptures.

Jehovah spoke!

A mighty blast rocked the glade. Its force fell on the stunned men there and pressed them to the ground. Veshtak flew in the air and fell ten paces away, as flaming bits of spark and fire and smoke shot high into the sky. The blast knocked all the men in the oak glade to the ground. They were blinded by the fire's sparks, but mostly by the booming thrust of the explosion.

The men were awestruck as they and their squires lay on the grass.

Then horns sounded, and the men of Dušan returned. They sang a song of Christian praise in the old tune of a pagan hymn with new words, saying, "God is great! Bless his holy name, and his son the Christ!"

The astonished followers of Veshtak lay helpless, stunned by the explosion unlike anything any of them had heard before, save during the worst thunderstorms raging in the high heavens.

They could do nothing but submit to the Christians—and the threat of hammers they bore. And each was baptized as he lay in the grass. When they arose to stand, they were Christians.

Veshtak came to himself and sat up. He looked around him and saw his flock being converted without resistance. The priest Erhard, attended by Dušan, was going among them and giving them sips of wine and biscuit, and praying over them.

This power of—something—was not to be denied.

Veshtak, his ears ringing, found his staff, staggered into the trackless forest and left our land. He never regained all of his hearing, and he later turned up as a Christian priest himself. He delivered his sermons in a loud and forceful voice, no doubt because his hearing was reduced. Veshtak retained his ways of decrying people's sins, demanding penance, scourging, and pain.

Some will always want a leader who demands such of them, even demeaning them. Some accept and even welcome it.

***

Dušan no longer served as a priest. Christian priests like Erhard were learned in the new faith, and most used their scriptures to lead people toward the paths of love and honest fairness most men seek. Dušan left the forge and kilns to his apprentices. Kamil and Bratumil had learned his crafts well, and they still do our iron making today with their own apprentices.

Dušan and his dog Král went into the forest near where I saw him that noontime by the cave. There he built a rude shelter, and in time welcomed others of a simple Christian faith to join him as brothers, to work out the best way to live their new lives, adapting their grasp of the mysteries of nature to their new religion.

Their little settlement is known as an outpost of monks. They study scriptures, chant their prayers, and work the land and forest in simplicity.

These monks learned the process of drawing spirits from fruit, using oil lamps to heat bowls of fermented plum juice. Cooler bowls of water suspended over them capture the dew formed by the rising vapors.

They became somewhat known for this spirit of fruit, as well as their simple piety.

***

I regularly traveled in a party of armed men from Budeč to Hrad Boleslav and other places with my administrators to oversee creation of our new defenses. I renovated and rebuilt the palace in Prague, and fortified it into the castle with new stone walls you see about you today. I built more fortified castles as well.

On one such journey to the northern edges of our lands, we came upon a monastery I had never visited.

The humble stone buildings were Frankish in design, walled and thatched, and monks there spoke both Czech and German. Women were there as well, kept separate from the monks who worked the fields and the apiaries. The women served in bakeries, gardens, the dairy of cows and goats. Mostly, they were older women who had retired from secular life to spend their days in wholesome labor and prayer.

As we approached the settlement, a bell toned. Workers ceased their labors and left their charges of field and stock. Some filed past me and my party to buildings where they would wash, pray, eat, pray again, and sleep, to gain strength for their next day of work and prayers.

One woman who tended the dairy, gray-haired and toothless like most of the females, had left her bovines and she glanced up at me. I recognized her.

"Saskia." I spoke her name quietly, and she turned fully toward me.

This old woman, a shadow of my nursemaid, was in her seventh decade, and lean. She seemed at peace.

She looked into my eyes and smiled. She said, "Hello, my princeling."

In an instant, the hours she had tended me returned, the rhyming games we played, even my hours at her warm breast, and I spoke to her. "I am glad to see you are well, Saskia. Milk Sister."

Her smile was warm and kind. Her face was ancient, yet at peace.

"In Christ I have put aside my old name, and taken the name of Magdalena," she said. The name of a saint who knew and loved Jesus.

My old bones lifted, and I stepped from the stirrup and embraced her.

Her story of how she had become a slave returned to me. The killing of her household, her lost son. How many stories there are like hers! Yet she survived and overcame the world's dangers, most of them, to finally find this place of solace. A place of peace, labor, love and prayer. What all men want!

After the briefest moment of mutual warmth, she stepped from me and said, "I may not touch or come close to any man. My vows do not permit it. Even of a beloved little child I knew in my youth. Even of you, Duke Boleslav."

We stood apart and looked into each other's faces—remembering, knowing, sharing.

"Sister Magdalena, your labors in the service of Christ will guarantee your soul's salvation." I don't know if I really believe that, but many do. I want to believe it. I must.

In her life of pain and woe, she found a path that could soothe her. If it is somehow all true, and she enters the heavenly gates to live with Jesus and the saints, I fear she will never see me there.

That is up to you, Kristián.

I know the way of Jesus, his teachings, are the ways to… well, peace, if not perhaps eternal joy. But who am I to say? I do not claim holiness.

I am mortal and weak, descended from a simple farmer whose work boots I viewed when I took my brother's throne.

I have done my best to do good, to redeem myself. I led my people to the new religion. Of any faith I might have chosen, this one is good, better than the old one whose gods demand too many sacrifices of blood.

I build churches, establish monasteries and convents. I support holy orders, erect shrines.

I strengthen my nation to withstand attack from our enemies. I clear our country of pagans, and help increase the people's bounty. I uphold the judicial reforms of my brother Václav.

I hope someday I may be seen as a good duke, or even as king, as I rely on no one over me in the care of my people.

Do I dream of salvation? I take a sip from the cup, wine from vineyards my grandmother planted, and with each sip I pray to the gods, or rather God, that I can be forgiven.

Kristián, Son, I am putting all my hopes on you. Learn everything you can about this Christian religion, and use it to persuade God to save me, if you can.

I weep for myself.

I have repented; I have spent long nights praying to the Christian god, and ache to believe I can be forgiven.

I have scourged myself. I've sent money to the bishop in Regensburg, and to Rome. I have built orphanages and charity houses.

But I know I will never be called "Good Duke Boleslav." They will hate me as a fratricide, the murderer of my perfect brother. The people's grandchildren will know me as criminal, and evil because of my dreadful act. I will be called "Boleslav the Heartless," "The Rash," "The Cruel."

Václav, you ask? Will they remember him as a good king? Many may call him such. He was not ideal as a ruler, though he was a good man. Unlike me. The best I can wish is to be forgotten by my descendants, except for the churches I build.

Václav though, they will remember him, and venerate him.

He was more than good. Václav, my dear brother Wenceslas.

Wenceslas was a saint.

A church bell rang just as Father ended his tale to me.

The duke had drunk his fill that night, and he began to weep. He lay his hand over his heart where he had wiped the blood of his brother a dozen years earlier. His little dog leapt from my lap onto that of his master, now falling into a sad slumber.

The fire had burned low, and the room began to chill. Tira stood by the hallway ready to help his duke to bed. I was ready to go to my room and prepare for my morning's journey.

Before I left him in his despairing sleep, I spoke a few words from the Psalms over my father, perhaps for his comfort, surely for mine, and perhaps for his salvation:

"Out of the depths I call to you, Lord!

Listen to my voice, to my cry for help.

Lord, if you kept an account of iniquities, who could stand?

But with you there is forgiveness, so that you may be revered.

I wait, I wait and put my hope in the Lord's word.

For there is faithful love with the Lord, and with him is redemption in abundance.

From the depths I cried to thee my voice Lord, do Thou hear!

Unto my pleas for mercy, I pray attend Thine ear."

I backed away as Father lay in weary anguish, tightly grasping in his fist the amulet hung around his neck, the shining vein of gold within a polished crystal.

Tira drew near, his conspirator in betrayal and in penitence. His careworn face gave me a glance and a somber nod as he went to help his friend the duke to bed.

***

I will turn my eyes to the Church, and my will to long labors for Father's salvation.

Whether my prayers will help Father, I don't know. But it is my duty, my life's work. I will pray for Father to find a way to salvation through the holy scriptures, the faith of Václav, and of Ludmila—and also, now, the faith of my father Duke Boleslav I of Bohemia.

A good king.

BIBLIOGRAPHY

Books Referenced for the Novel:

The Origin of Christianity in Bohemia
Marvin Kantor

Old Czech Legends
Alois Jirasek

Good King Wenceslas—The Real Story
Jan Reizl

From Good King Wenceslas to the Good Soldier Svejk—A Dictionary of Czech Popular Culture
Andrew Roberts

The Chronicle of the Czechs
Cosmas of Prague

Máj (various translations)
Karel Hynek Mácha

"Bay Psalm Book," or "The Whole Booke of Psalmes, Faithfully Translated into English Metre."
1640 edition

Scholarly Papers:

The Archeology of the Dawn of Prague
-Ivana Boháčová

Slavic Pagan World

-Compilation by Garry Green

Ritual and Cultural Change—Transformations in Rituals at the Junction of Pagan Religion and Christianity in Early Medieval Poland
-Justyna Baron

Swords Uncovered at the Burial Ground of the Stará Kouřim Stronghold (9th century) from the Perspective of Archaeology and Metallography
-Jiří Hošek

Early Medieval Lead Processing in The Slavic territories and The Possible Mention of Trade in Lead by Ibrahim Ibn Yaqub
-Dariusz Rozmus

Websites:

Wikipedia.org

CzechCenter.org

MyCatholic.life

Thoughtco.com

BehindTheName.com

TresBohemes.com

Get-To-Know-Cz.tumblr.com

TopTablePlanner.com

Translate.Google.com expats.cz biblegateway.com

"Good King Wenceslas"

From "Oxford Book of Carols"

1853, Attributed to John Mason Neale

Good King Wences'las looked out, on the Feast of Stephen,

When the snow lay round about, deep and crisp and even;

Brightly shone the moon that night, tho' the frost was cruel,

When a poor man came in sight, gath'ring winter fuel.

"Hither, page, and stand by me, if thou know'st it, telling,

Yonder peasant, who is he? Where and what his dwelling?"

"Sire, he lives a good league hence, underneath the mountain;

Right against the forest fence, by Saint Agnes' fountain."

"Bring me flesh, and bring me wine, bring me pine logs hither:

Thou and I shall see him dine, when we bear them thither."

Page and monarch, forth they went, forth they went together;

Through the rude wind's wild lament and the bitter weather.

"Sire, the night is darker now, and the wind blows stronger;

Fails my heart, I know not how; I can go no longer."

"Mark my footsteps, good my page. Tread thou in them boldly.

Thou shalt find the winter's rage freeze thy blood less coldly."

In his master's steps he trod, where the snow lay dinted;

Heat was in the very sod which the saint had printed.

Therefore, Christian men, be sure, wealth or rank possessing,

Ye who now will bless the poor, shall yourselves find blessing.

ABOUT THE AUTHOR

George WB Scott is an East Tennessee video producer and videographer with a life-long interest in European and American history. Scott was born in Stuart, Florida, and graduated from Martin County High School. He attended Guilford College in Greensboro, North Carolina, and graduated from Appalachian State University with a cum laude degree in Communications, and concentrations in Theater and Broadcasting. Scott has written a full-length science fiction screenplay, a childhood memoir, and a 140,000-word historical novel set in Charleston, South Carolina, during the American Civil War. He lives with his wife Mary Leidig in Knoxville, Tennessee. They have two sons, Daniel and Gideon.

OTHER TITLES BY GEORGE WB SCOTT

I Jonathan, A Charleston Tale of the Rebellion

Growing Up In Eden

NOTE FROM GEORGE WB SCOTT

Word-of-mouth is crucial for any author to succeed. If you enjoyed *The Good King*, please leave a review online—anywhere you are able. Even if it's just a sentence or two. It would make all the difference and would be very much appreciated.

Thanks!
George WB Scott

We hope you enjoyed reading this title from:

BLACK ROSE
writing™

www.blackrosewriting.com

Subscribe to our mailing list – *The Rosevine* – and receive **FREE** books, daily deals, and stay current with news about upcoming releases and our hottest authors.
Scan the QR code below to sign up.

Already a subscriber? Please accept a sincere thank you for being a fan of Black Rose Writing authors.

View other Black Rose Writing titles at
www.blackrosewriting.com/books and use promo code
PRINT to receive a **20% discount** when purchasing.